The Diane Game

When Ann Lanagan, a reporter for a small-town newspaper, drives off to pick up her sister Diane at the airport, she has no idea that she is headed for a web of intrigue that will threaten her personal identity—and her life.

Ann and Diane are twins; both beautiful, yet Ann is prudent and unadventurous, while Diane is reckless and exuberant. As children, Ann and Diane had played often at switching identities to confuse the grown-ups. But when Diane is killed in a car crash on the way back from the airport, Ann cannot resist the temptation of her sister's exciting life, the suitcase full of glamorous clothes, and the airline ticket with the open return to San Francisco. She decides once again to play the Diane game—this time for good.

The consequences of the switch are more than Ann bargained for. She finds herself involved in an industrial spy ring dealing with the syndicate, even making love to a stranger in a pile of hundred-dollar bills. Nor is Ann prepared for the ultimate, chilling consequence of the Diane game: that by pretending to be Diane, she actually becomes Diane.

Also by Stanley Cohen

The abduction (1971)

STANLEY COHEN

The Diane Game

constable crime

Constable London

First published in Great Britain 1974
by Constable & Company Ltd
10 Orange Street London WC2H 7EG
Copyright © Stanley Cohen 1973

ISBN 0 09 460420 7

Author's note to members of
the computer industry
If the events described in this book
should ever actually be tried and found
to be effective and useful, please
remember, you saw it here first.

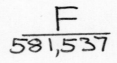

F
—————
581,537

Printed and bound in Great Britain by
REDWOOD BURN LIMITED
Trowbridge & Esher

11/74

To Nat and Sid
and all the rest of the family and
friends of Mighty O Foundation

1

Totally out of breath, she stopped hurrying as she entered the terminal building. She glanced around and spotted a clock. Diane's flight was due at 9:12 and it was 9:05. She had just enough time to make it to the gate.

She paused to catch her breath and get her bearings. The terminal was new to her. She had heard about it and seen photographs, but the vaulting, soaring lines and curves, streaming off in all sorts of crazy directions, seemed a glimpse into tomorrow.

Her sweeping gaze came to rest on a huge, futuristically sculptured mass growing out of the floor and, in one face of it, a table of letters and numbers, some of which abruptly began to reel and spin with little clicking sounds. A digital schedule board. She walked over in front of it. Flight 46 from San Francisco, due at 9:12, DELAYED. She could relax. The frantic rush had been unnecessary. But she could not have taken a chance. Not after reading Diane's letter.

She went up to the counter under the schedule board, where two crisp ground hostesses answered questions with practiced courtesy. "Pardon me," she said to one of them. "Your flight 46 from San Francisco. Do you know how long it will be delayed?"

"I'm afraid we haven't received word yet about estimated time of arrival. Takeoff was delayed because of an equipment problem, but it did get off. And as of now, all arrivals here are running behind because of the weather and air traffic buildup."

"Do you have *any* idea how long it might be?"

"Well, you should keep an eye on the flight announcements," the hostess said, pointing at the board. "It could improve, but I frankly think it will be at least two hours."

"Thank you." She walked away from the counter. Two hours or more, probably more.

She began looking around again. Plenty of time for exploring. As she walked and turned and gazed, it occurred to her that every line seemed designed to project a sense of motion and flight. The terminal was a giant bird, poised to flap its molded concrete wings and propel itself into the air. Saarinen. One of his many masterpieces.

She walked up the wide steps in the center of the terminal, studying the structure, particularly the marvelously sleek little overhead catwalk, so deftly contoured to flow into the walls of the building. She reached the top of the stairs and moved into the seating area, taking a seat opposite the sloping glass wall that looked out over the airfield.

It was an ugly night. The light rain was still falling and the mist seemed to be getting worse. The drive down the Sawmill River Parkway had been unnerving, in fact, treacherous. And if the mist continued to thicken it would certainly be worse going back. The giant planes moved around the field in slow motion like huge, silent aluminum specters. She looked around at the others in the seating area, some reading, some restless, others obviously accustomed to spending time in airline terminals on bad nights.

Diane. Diane knew airplanes and jetports as part of her way of life. At least one assumed so. How did Diane really live? How did she keep herself occupied? Apparently she had never been lured into marriage. Of course not. Much too confining.

She opened her bag and took out Diane's letter. Expensive stationery, tasteful and unscented. She would have almost expected something wildly scented.

Dear Ann,

I hope getting this doesn't startle you too much. It has been a while, hasn't it? How are you and how've you been and what's new and all that? As you can guess, your kid sister by a half hour is writing for the first time in years because she wants to ask for something.

Ann, I've gotten myself embroiled in a spectacular tangle of affairs and I need to talk to someone outside the circle of creeps and misfits I've gathered around myself. They're fun, but for serious conversation I need someone real. And someone who can listen objectively. I know this sounds crazy, Ann, but I want to come and talk to you, to come home and spend some time with you. Suddenly, no one else will do. It's been a long-ass time. It shouldn't have been this long but it has.

I've booked a seat on TWA flight 46, landing at JFK at 9:12 P.M. Friday. Let me know if this is okay. I hope to hell it is. In fact, it's got to be. But let me know, so I won't get to New York and not be able to find you because you're in Tahiti or in Kenya on safari or somewhere.

Friday.

Love,
Di

She folded the letter carefully along the original creases, slid it back into the envelope, and stuffed it into the pocket of her slacks. She glanced at her watch. Still essentially the same two hours to wait.

What could possibly have prompted Diane to make such a dramatic call for help? Man problems? Never. Not Diane. Since receiving the letter, she had wondered at length about the nature of Diane's "spectacular tangle of affairs."

Certainly there was nothing in her own orderly life that could ever lead to a "spectacular tangle of affairs." Five days a week in and out of the *Reporter Dispatch* office on Main Street. Meeting deadlines. So much ado about so very little. And then, shopping on Saturdays and *The New York Times* on Sundays. The *Times* and Roger—her own affair, hardly spectacular. "Routine" might be a better word. Handsome, lovable, devoted Roger. Almost dashing, especially holding a nine iron, or on skis. But really a little too predictable.

Even her vacatious had become part of the pattern. The trip that had ended that morning was a typical example. A week by herself at a Pocono resort which featured "resident physician" in its ad copy. She had kept Roger from coming with her. She had spent most of the week thinking about Diane and the letter and how someone gets herself embroiled in a spectacular tangle of affairs.

There had to be some way to change things. She'd thought about inviting herself to move to San Francisco and live with Diane, and assumed she would be welcome. "Think how devastating it would be, Diane. The Lanigan twins reunited. I could sell the house in Mount Kisco and contribute piles of money to the kitty. Imagine the Bay Area being terrorized by the Lanigan look-alikes. I know that I've never been as free-spirited as you, Diane, but from now on. . . ." Diane wouldn't want that, of course. Not really. But things were going to change in Ann Lanigan's life, with or without her sister's help.

She got up and walked around, wandering finally up the stairs to the coffee shop. After ordering a cup of coffee, she asked herself what Diane would do at that exact same moment. She had always thought of this mental exercise as the Diane game. Like most twins, she and Diane as children had switched identities on occasion, just for the fun of it. Now, years after, she continued to compare the way she did things to the way she imagined Diane might do them. If Diane had two hours to wait, Diane might just *not* wait. Or she might go into the cocktail lounge rather than the coffee shop.

"Hello."

She looked up. He had a warm smile and was wearing a blazer and turtleneck. "Hello."

"You seemed miles away," he said.

"In a sense, I was."

"You waiting to take off or for someone to arrive?"

"I'm meeting my sister."

"Is she as beautiful as you?"

"She's an identical twin."

"No fooling. I ought to get a friend and come back and wait with you."

"I'm afraid we're going straight home as soon as she arrives."

He hesitated, then smiled. "Could you be trying to tell me something?"

"I hope you aren't offended. Nothing personal."

"Be sure and give your sister my regards."

"I'll do that."

As he walked away, she felt a flush of regret and began replaying the incident in terms of the Diane game. Diane would have enjoyed his interest, probably joined him for a drink, very likely seen him again. Things like this came so easily to her

She thought about the man. He was attractive, but somehow she couldn't quite make herself respond warmly. She had put him down hard. Diane's way was better, certainly more interesting. She wished she could do it over. She even considered going to look for him, to tell him, Yes, find a friend for Diane and come back.

She suddenly realized how much she wanted to see her twin. Diane was coming to talk? Well, she was also coming to listen, and advise, and maybe help her older sister shed the cocoon and start flying a little.

She paid her check and walked back to the schedule board. Names and numbers were spinning, but flight 46 just sat there. DELAYED. The clock read 10:05. She wandered over to a newsstand and, after scanning the magazines, pulled out a *Harper's*. She had already received it by subscription, but she chose it anyway. Diane would have probably selected *Playboy*. Or the *Cosmopolitan* with the lead article about the sixteen newly discovered erogenous zones. Maybe she would, too. Next time. No! Enough next time! Next time was now! She put back the *Harper's* and bought the *Playboy*, which promised a story by Isaac Bashevis Singer and a provocative interview.

She returned to the seating area and found a seat facing the glass wall. The mist seemed a little thicker, but visibility was obviously still adequate since planes continued moving around. Hopefully, the condition would hold a little longer. She would hate the frustration and delay of having Diane's flight diverted to Boston or somewhere.

Thumbing through the magazine, she came to the centerfold and glanced briefly at the photo, the Hefner selection, the future star. Wasn't the girl a trifle over-developed for stardom? She was certainly nothing that would eclipse Ann and Diane, the fabulous Lanigan twins of Mount Kisco, the loveliest, most identical pair of girls ever seen in those parts, ask anyone, crown jewels of the club and the countryside, the renowned daughters of Quick Sam and Louise Lanigan, and mirror images besides—at least, until you talked to them a bit. So alike to see and so different to know. Yet anyone who did know them would tell you that despite their surprisingly different natures, they were always close and were frequently seen together, recognizable at a distance with their long straight brown hair, their familiar trademark. Seeing them was like blurred double vision, a pleasantly startling experience for the beholder. And you could still find one of them almost any time by simply dropping in at the little gray-painted brick offices of the *Reporter Dispatch* on Main Street in Mount Kisco.

She glanced at her watch. Ten-thirty. Unable to get into any of the stories or articles in the magazine, she got up to check the schedule board again. Flight 46 was due to arrive at eleven o'clock.

She went back and sat down. How long *had* it been since she had seen Diane? Five years? Not since Aunt Flossie's funeral, which was almost six years ago. Aunt Flossie, the last of their common roots. She and Diane had drifted apart with college, she going to Simmons and Diane to Berkeley, then seeing each other Christmases and summers. They had traveled together for one summer, to Europe after their freshman year.

After graduation and their twenty-first birthday, the estate was divided and Diane returned to her beloved San Francisco to settle. She stayed home and took a job writing local news for the Mount Kisco page of the White Plains *Reporter Dispatch* to keep herself occupied for a while. The "for a while" had already amounted to nearly seven years. She suddenly wished she'd never have to enter that cluttered office again. Let someone else cover town meetings and club meetings and all the rest of it.

She looked at her watch. Ten forty-five. She checked the schedule board once more and, noting the gate number, she walked back up the steps and into the corridor leading to the gate area. Something about the long, sleek, tubular enclosure made her feel engulfed and isolated. Was that spooky tube symbolic as it rose in the middle and fell, so that the end was never in sight of the beginning? In a way, she hoped so.

The accident happened as they were driving home from the airport. They were on the Sawmill, just north of the junction with the Cross County Parkway. Diane had insisted on driving, and neither had fastened a seat belt. The road was wet from the light rain and visibility poor. As Diane was taking a sharp curve on the almost deserted parkway, a squat, rampant sports car pulled out to pass them. Then, suddenly, one, two, three deer were in front of them. And at that precise moment, the bright lights from a single car coming from the opposite direction threw up fuzzy circles of blinding light, silhouetting the deer.

There was no place to go. Diane tried braking, went into a skid, missed the curve, hit the raised edge of the road, and overturned. The car rolled over and down an embankment. It tumbled into a steep ravine, overturned again, and finally stopped when it piled into a railroad freight car, one of several on a deserted siding.

Somehow thrown clear when the car had overturned the second time, she got to her feet and staggered toward the car, tripping over something familiar. Diane's bulky shoulder bag with the ornate brass clasp. As she picked it up and moved forward again, a small pop of flame sputtered to life on the car's engine. The car stood right side up, its hood torn away. She could see Diane, pinned in the front seat and still.

Fearful that the car might explode, she backed away and hesitated for several minutes, watching the flame as if hypnotized. Then she rushed to the window. Diane was lifeless, her head hanging to one side at an unnatural angle, her eyes open and glazed, the steering wheel pressed against her chest.

She screamed and moved back from the car, staring at Diane's limply hanging head, and kept moving backward until she bumped into a tree. She slid to the ground without taking her eyes off Diane and the car and the flame. She began to sob, quietly at first, then hysterically.

She stopped crying and stared in silence at the wreckage. Hearing car doors open and close, she jumped up and plunged farther back into the underbrush to wait and watch.

Two state highway troopers climbed down the side of the ravine, each carrying a large flashlight. The fire in the front end had gone out. They approached the wreckage and moved over and around and in and out of the carcass of the dead car like dogs nosing a dump for morsels of food. They checked the ground around the car.

One of the troopers went back up the hill toward the parkway and disappeared. He reappeared after a few minutes and the two troopers stood by the wreckage, talking and occasionally checking something in or on the car. She continued her stony vigil, squatting a safe distance away, unnoticed in the thickening fog, still clutching Diane's bag. They would need the bag for identification. She should take it to them, tell them how the accident happened—without, of course, letting them see the bag's contents.

She heard more car doors and voices. More people came down the embankment. A flashbulb illuminated the area around the car, and she caught a glimpse of Diane's head. Then another flashbulb, and another. Little explosions of light. Another and another and another.

Two sets of headlights approached, coming slowly around the far end of the freight cars, the light beams dancing and swaying as the two vehicles bumped over the railroad tracks. One vehicle was a wrecker, festooned with revolving lights which filled the area with pulsing illumination. The other was an ambulance, moving quietly. No siren or whistles or bells.

The wreckage was surrounded by a crowd of men, two from the wrecker, two from the ambulance, several troopers. They were struggling with Diane's body, pinned in the car. The wrecker pulled in front of the car, blocking her view of Diane. She watched as the men worked with chains at the back of the truck and listened as its engine whined with power. The wrecked car jerked and shook a time or two, then moved forward a little so that she could see Diane, laid out on a stretcher. One of the men bent over her, checking and examining. He stood up and another man pulled a sheet completely over her head.

"The wrong handbag is in the car," Ann whispered softly as they loaded the stretcher into the ambulance, backed up, turned around and drove it slowly away, over the bumpy tracks and around the far end of the rail cars.

All but two of the troopers left. The two remaining troopers watched as the wrecker began its departure, joggling over the tracks and disappearing. Then the two troopers climbed back up the embankment to the parkway. She heard their car start and pull away. She was alone, crouched in wet underbrush in an unknown spot somewhere off the Sawmill Parkway, staring into a thickening fog at the hazy outline of two railroad cars.

She climbed back to the edge of the parkway and began walking, just off the pavement, south toward New York, still clutching Diane's bag. An occasional car zipped by. Each one startled her. The headlights seemed to materialize suddenly in the fog which also muffled the oncoming sound. Where was she? What time was it? Her body felt wet, soaked through, totally disheveled, and completely broken by a network of small but angry pains.

After she had been walking for what seemed a very long time, she noticed a glow ahead and to the left. A stationary source of light. Watching it brighten as she moved toward it, she finally saw that it was a service station, not too far from a ramp leading off the parkway.

Coming to the ramp, she started down it and toward the station. As she reached the hardtop apron, which held several parked cars, she ducked behind the first one, which was empty, to survey things. The next car, a station wagon, had a man in front and children sleeping in the back.

She finally stepped out from behind the car and started walking briskly toward the station, trying to walk naturally, and as she approached, she saw it! The wrecker, her car still suspended, and a trooper standing next to it, talking to a mechanic. She hesitated, feeling weak, and as she did the trooper looked at her. She resumed her natural pace as best she could and continued walking toward them.

She came within earshot and heard "Lanigan" and "Mount Kisco" among the dialogue. She looked down at Diane's bag in her hand and, without hesitating again, walked on by them into the station. Then she began to tremble. Once inside the station she looked around for the ladies' room. It wasn't there. Probably outside. And no one inside to ask.

As she went back out, the trembling became worse, almost uncontrollable. She glanced at the trooper, who studied her as if she looked familiar, She walked around to the side of the building but could find no rest rooms. She followed the concrete walk all the way back to the rear of the station, looked down along the back side of the building, and saw no doors. Where was it? She began to shake almost violently. She couldn't remember ever having felt that weak before.

She took a couple of deep breaths. A few moments later, she walked back around to the front and directly up to the trooper and mechanic, who was holding the copy of *Playboy* from the car. As she approached, the trooper was saying, ". . . have to check everything with fatalities, so call us when you get the trunk open. . . ."

"Pardon me," she said to the mechanic. "Where's the ladies' room?"

"Around this side, over here. You went the wrong way before."

"Thank you."

"What on earth happened to you?" the trooper asked.

"I fell and skinned my knee. I'll be all right."

"Can I give you a hand with that knee? I've got some first-aid stuff in the car."

"No, really. I'll be fine. It isn't bad."

"You sure, now?"

"Yes. Really."

He smiled. "You know, I must be losing my mind. Or maybe it's this late shift that's getting me. But I feel like I've seen you somewhere."

"Just a funny coincidence, I suppose." She started toward the rest rooms.

"I think there's somebody in there right now," the mechanic said.

"I'll wait," she said, and kept walking. She heard the trooper say," Jeez, she sure looks familiar."

She walked up next to the door to the rest room

and leaned against the wall. She was trembling again. A young man came out of the adjacent men's room and nodded at her. She tried to nod back.

The sound of the toilet being flushed came through the transom over the door. She clenched her fists, hoping whoever was in there wouldn't dawdle too long. Finally, a woman came out and headed for the row of parked cars. She ducked into the grimy, poorly lit cubicle, slammed the door, and twisted the lock. Then she slid to the floor.

"Will you be much longer?" The voice was sharp and impatient. She did not know how long she had been slumped there.

"Just a couple of minutes."

She opened Diane's bag and, seeing the two brown envelopes Diane had told her about, pulled out the fat one, so fat it was almost square, opened the end flap, and shook the contents down into her hand. Thick, banded clumps of new one-hundred-dollar bills. She looked around, glanced up at the transom, pushed the money back into the envelope, and burrowed the envelope deep into the recesses of the bag. She took out the other envelope, which was sealed, but this was hardly the time to examine its contents. She lifted out Diane's bulky wallet and riffled through it. Money, more than she would ever carry, credit cards, driver's license, a checkbook, bits of paper with names, numbers, and other notations, a scratch pad of perforated sheets, and several business cards with men's names. She snapped the wallet closed and pushed it down in the bag. She took out the airline ticket. The return-trip line was marked "open." The pulse in her throat began to accelerate to a point that made her feel choked.

More irritated slapping on the door. "Be right out," she said and got to her feet. She smoothed her hair several times with her hand and unlocked the door. The woman, holding the hand of a half-asleep little girl, glared at her and led the child past her into the rest room. "Sorry I was so long," she said to the woman and started toward the front of the station.

The trooper was gone. The mechanic had backed the wrecker and her car to a far corner of the paved area and was disengaging them.

She walked by the gas pumps toward the street and the parkway. She tried to walk naturally but found this harder and harder to do as the pain throughout her body continued to intensify. Her head throbbed; her left ankle was twisted. A hole was torn out of her slacks, the skid on the knee having taken cloth, and, judging from the stinging pain, a little flesh. Her shoes were a mess.

She walked onto the road, under the parkway, and up the ramp to the southbound lane. Once out of sight of the station, she gave in to the pain and began to limp and whimper softly as she walked.

Back on the parkway, she turned to face the traffic, but saw no cars. Visibility was poor, though the sky seemed to be getting lighter. Finally, two headlights. She held out a thumb, something she had never done before in her entire life.

The car slowed down and stopped a few yards down the road. She turned and limped toward it. An old car, two young couples, all freaky-looking kids, the couple in back huddled, intertwined, and apparently asleep. "Get in front," said the girl next to the kid driving. "The two in back are out of it. No use disturbing them."

She climbed in.

"Where're you trying to get to?" asked the boy driving. He had long stringy hair and a heavy growth of beard and mustache.

"The airport," she said. "Kennedy."

"Really? From here? Now?"

"Yes."

"Do you hitch much?" the girl asked, looking her over.

"Not too often." She wouldn't have put it past Diane, however. Diane!

"Just out of curiosity," said the boy at the wheel, "you didn't plan your day's activities to include hitching to Kennedy at five in the morning?"

"Not exactly. I . . . I was in a . . . a minor accident. And I left my car at the station back there."

The girl glanced at her knee. "You all right?" The girl seemed genuinely concerned but anxious not to appear too inquisitive.

"I'm okay. A little sore. The car's in bad shape." She tightened her grip on Diane's bag.

"Wouldn't the pigs help you get where you were going?" he asked.

"I guess I really didn't give them the chance."

"We're going into the city. We can give you a lift into the city and you can get a cab or something out to Kennedy from there."

"I'd appreciate it very much."

"We're glad to do it. The shoe's usually on the other foot."

"Usually is right," added the girl.

They continued driving for a while in silence. She tried to identify the odor in the car. It was a little bit familiar, perhaps, but not quite identifiable. A smell suggestive of barnyards. Unwashed bodies? Marijuana? What if it was marijuana and they were stopped and searched? She obviously wasn't one of them. What could her story possibly be? What if it was the same trooper? . . . The thick brown envelope . . . What if these kids turned on her? She began to tremble again.

"You sure you're all right?" asked the girl.

"I think so. I guess I'm still upset from the accident."

"Would you, uh, do you think you'd like to smoke something?"

"I don't smoke."

"Would you like something to drink? A beer? We've got some beer."

A beer? At five in the morning? She'd hardly tasted any since college. "Do you have an extra beer?"

"Sure." The girl twisted around, leaned over the seat, fumbled with things on the floor in back and finally straightened around with a can of beer. "Want me to open it for you?"

"If you don't mind."

The girl yanked the tab and handed her the can. It was not icy but still cool. She took a long triple swallow. It tasted wonderful.

They drove along in silence for a while. She downed the first half of the can hungrily and then slowed down to just sipping it. At one point the couple in back shifted positions, mumbling to one another as they did. The sky continued to brighten through the light fog, which seemed to be breaking slightly. Holding her beer can, she watched the familiar scenery close to the road, the Sawmill, the Henry Hudson, the underside of the George Washington Bridge, the West Side Highway. She offered to pay the two tolls, but they refused her.

They pulled off at the Forty-sixth Street ramp and found her a cab. "Give me the can," the girl said, taking the empty from her. "Don't pollute this city any worse than it already is."

She thanked them profusely and got out. The two in back were just waking up. After getting into the cab, she watched their car pull away, heading further south.

As the taxi headed across Manhattan, she began reviewing her decision. She could still turn back. She watched quietly as the early-morning scenery moved by them and the taxi continued on its uninterrupted course.

When she arrived at the airline terminal, she had the ticket validated for flight 585, the first flight out, which left at eight o'clock. She went up to the coffee shop, where she was the first customer of the day. She sat down and had coffee, and a refill, and another. The place looked familiar. The man with the turtleneck and blazer, just nine or ten hours before . . . where was he, now that she could use a friend? She had no one. She glanced at her watch. It had stopped at 12:30.

For the second time in a matter of hours she was walking through the strange corridor, toward the planes, alone. This time the trek seemed endless, like walking on a treadmill inside a capsule, until she finally reached the crest in the middle of it and the far end came into view. She held Diane's shoulder bag in place with her right hand and carried the airline ticket in her left.

The incredible night was over. She had to hurry to San Francisco, a place she hardly knew, to sit in totally strange surroundings and wait for a telephone call that would invite her to her own funeral.

2

The plane continued to climb until it finally broke out
of the muck and into the dazzling brilliance of morning
above the weather. It's always a perfect day when you're
far enough off the ground.

She sat in her seat by the window and watched as
the weather changed in layers. The sun and sky made
her feel warmer and a little better. She'd had the sensation of having committed herself totally and irrevocably,
as the plane left the ground.

There was so much to sort out in her head and so
little time to do it. Every detail and circumstance had
fallen too neatly into place. She had been pushed. Some
force, somewhere, had set the whole thing into motion.

No doubt in the clear, cool light of day, calm, level-headed Ann would have handled the situation with a businesslike respect for keeping the truth on track. But the accident and the fog and the deer and, finally, the moment of decision at the service station when she decided the truth wasn't really that important . . . one shove after another, and it had happened. Ann was dead. Diane lived.

She had been leaving for a week in the Poconos when she received Diane's letter. Everyone knew she was going away. No one knew she'd returned. She'd unpacked and then left again to go meet Diane. The luggage in the trunk would be taken as her own. And Diane, in the stillness of death, would portray her perfectly.

She thought about the way people had stared at the two of them in the airport. After all those years, they looked more alike than ever. Even their hair, still the same. Oh, precious Diane!

Her eyes stung, and she pushed her thoughts to the house in Mount Kisco. Someone would find Tony a new home. Tony, her mixed-breed dog, her rebellion against purebred snobbery, and Felix, her black-and-white kitten. Mr. Hodgeson would see to them. Sweet, mild, little Mr. Hodgeson at the bank, dedicated friend of Sam Lanigan, executor of Sam's will and now hers, would dispose of the house and the contents and the pets, arrange her funeral and get the estate totaled up and take his little commission and transfer the whole thing to her sister, Diane, in San Francisco.

As the stewardess leaned over to offer breakfast, she crossed her legs to cover the skinned knee showing through the hole in the slacks. The man sitting in the aisle seat had glanced at it and looked back at her, studying her as if she looked slightly familiar. Did he know Diane? He would have said something if he did. She tried to dismiss it from her mind. She was getting paranoid. She unfolded her arms from around Diane's handbag and moved it from her lap to the empty seat next to her. No one was going to snatch her purse and run away with it on an airplane at thirty thousand feet. She let down the tray table and the stewardess handed her the tray.

While eating the grapefruit and orange sections, she found herself reconstructing the brief ride with Diane from JFK to the Sawmill River Parkway. "I think I'm in a lot of trouble," Diane had said. What kind of trouble? "It's so goddamn incredible, you won't believe it. You always knew your baby sister was wild. Wait till you hear what she's into, now."

Diane had teased a little more before getting started, but soon she was pouring out the details of a story at least as improbable as she had suggested it would be. Industrial espionage? "A more polite name for it is business intelligence." Diane the spy!

"It seemed like a lark at first, or a gag. Then, all of a sudden, they were talking money. Big money. And Jesus, have I been spending! I've spent myself to the point where I *have* to begin thinking about money. You stayed on the plantation, big sister. Nothing costs you anything. You've probably got Hodgeson handling things for you so that your half of Quick Sam's portfolio is growing. I moved to San Francisco and set up the kind of place I've always wanted, and now the money seems to be dwindling faster than I like to think about.

"Do you have any idea what I've got in my handbag?" Diane both asked and answered the question as they were crossing the Whitestone Bridge. "First, there's an envelope containing one thousand new one-hundred-dollar bills. That's a fat envelope. Then there's another envelope containing the elephant, which is what all the fuss is about. That's a thinner envelope. You might say I'm really into this thing. It's scary, but I have to admit it's just about the most exciting thing I've ever done." Diane's voice had reflected excitement and fascination of a high order. But there was also a strong undercurrent of fear.

She'd asked Diane about the legalities of the whole thing. "I was assured it wasn't cops and robbers or spies and agents," Diane had answered. "Strictly corporate. The only stake is money. Except that some corporations nowadays are becoming entangled with noncorporate organizations. Syndicates. And these syndicates don't kid around. They'd kill somebody for a lot less money than's in this envelope. That's the scary part . . ."

She finished what she could eat of the ham omelet and refused the stewardess's offer of more coffee. As she transferred the tray to the empty middle seat, the man on the aisle reached up and got her a pillow. Diane surely would have smiled at him.

She smiled and thanked him.

Getting comfortable with her seat tilted back and the pillow against the cabin wall, she took the handbag into her lap again. So much more to dredge up out of that hour's car ride and review. One of the problems, Diane had said, was that she was getting to like Beech a little too much. Beech? she'd asked Diane. Beecher Grant. The leak. And the pink Englishman was getting a little sticky with his presumptuousness. The pink Englishman? A contact and a friend. And the button man was beginning to threaten to act like a button man. Button man? A gorilla for the syndicate, Diane had explained. And the money and the elephant and Diane's life in San Francisco and the house on Lombard Street . . .

The fog was thickening. Big fuzzy balls of light and one, two, three deer in the road. No guardrail. Why no guardrail? Over and over and over and over . . . She woke up feeling drenched, wet as if rained on, not knowing how long she had been asleep. She buzzed for a stewardess. The man in the aisle seat was working out of his briefcase.

A stewardess appeared and flipped off the call light. "Can I help y u with something?"

"May I have more coffee?"

"Certainly."

"And could you get me a magazine?"

"Any one in particular?"

"Do you have a *Playboy*?"

"I'm sorry, no. Any other you'd like?"

The man in the aisle seat looked up from his work. "I have a *Playboy*. Want to read mine?"

"Thanks, yes."

He pulled the magazine out of his briefcase and handed it to her. "You know, you seemed to be having a bad dream while you were taking your little snooze."

"I must have been. It woke me up."

He began putting papers back in his briefcase.

"Don't let me keep you from your work," she said.

"Glad for the excuse to put it off till later. My name is John Sturdi."

"I'm Diane Lanigan. Do you live in San Francisco?"

"For the last seven years. Where do you live?"

"Lombard Street."

He nodded at the address. "Maybe we could get together for a drink some time."

"I'd like that." As she watched him jot her name and Lombard Street on a note pad in his wallet, she wondered if Diane had a listed or an unlisted telephone number.

3

The San Francisco sun was impossibly bright. She blinked her eyes and looked from side to side, absorbing the unfamiliar scenery as the taxi took her toward Lombard Street. Rummaging in Diane's bag, she found a key case. Several keys. To what?

When the taxi drew closer to the city, she asked the driver if they were going to cross the Golden Gate Bridge.

"We're coming up from the south," he said. "The Golden Gate's north of the city. This your first trip to San Francisco?"

"Well, no. I live here."

He deliberately stared into the rear-view mirror to get a good look at her.

"That is, I'm going to be living here."

"Like I said, this your first trip to San Francisco?"

"More or less."

He shrugged and seemed to retreat back into his own thoughts. She hardly blamed him. He represented a no-risk situation but she would have to be careful not to ask stupid questions of anyone who knew Diane. She was starting a whole new Diane game. Except that this time she wouldn't just play it inside her head. She'd be playing out in the open. And for big stakes. Diane had been quick. She'd have to be quicker. Much quicker.

They approached the city and she began studying the distinctive hillside architecture. Steep hills, steeper than she'd imagined. What would people do if it ever snowed?

Then into the city and onto the spectacular hills and the sensation of being hurled into space on carnival rides, in and out and around cable cars, through streets of shops and restaurants and hotels and onto more hills, row houses and townhouses and apartments, all brilliantly colorful in the morning sun ... Yes, Diane's beloved city did have an instant magic about it.

The taxi turned and she spotted a sign that said Lombard Street. The cabbie nosed the car down a steep hill and began moving slowly along, reading house numbers, finally stopping. She felt for a moment as if she were coming to visit. Then everything came flooding back and she had to take a deep breath to regain control.

She paid the large fare, thinking that it was a good thing she was inheriting a rich sister's estate, and got out of the taxi. She stood on the sidewalk and watched as the cab headed down the dizzying slope. Then she turned toward the house. Diane's house. Off-white stucco, trimmed in dark glossy wood, touched here and there with bright flowers and greens; a handsome bay window, two floors to the right and three floors to the left, to accommodate the staggering drop-off of the slope, the house wedged tightly between the houses on either side.

She reached the stoop and took out the key case. Then, before trying the first key, she pulled back her hand. What if someone was inside? She looked up and down the street. The cab had long disappeared with its driver, one of her two acquaintances in the city.

None of the keys wanted to penetrate the tiny opening, no doubt because her hand was shaking. She stopped struggling with the lock and leaned against the door frame to try and compose herself. Finally, she tried another key and it slid into place.

As she opened the door, she heard a whistling noise, a sound she would assume was a teakettle anywhere but in an empty house. She stepped inside and the sound became more pronounced. It had to be a teakettle.

"Oh, there you are." A male voice, distinctly British.

Her knees buckled. The game was under way. Who was he? What was Diane's relationship with him? How would Diane react to his presence? She would have to face this panic with every person she met.

"I won't ask where you've been all night," he said, still from the other room.

What would Diane say? Something glib, no doubt. "I should hope not," she managed, almost gagging on the words.

"I *could* ask, you know," he said.

"Doesn't mean you'd get an answer." That was better.

He walked into the living room and looked at her,

his expression registering no surprise. "I was brewing a pot of tea," he said. "You're just in time." He was holding a kitchen canister in his hand. He was chubby, with a florid complexion and overlong bluish-white hair, very wavy and full. Along with his ruffle-fronted shirt, he wore bellbottoms, a wide belt, and square-toed, silver-buckled shoes, an outfit that would have been a bit much on someone half his age. He had to be Diane's pink Englishman. "I had a devil of a time finding the tea," he said. And then, "My God, what happened to you?"

"A slight accident," she said.

"You look like you've been in a wreck. What happened to your knee?"

"I fell and skinned it. Nothing serious."

"Let's have tea. One thing I adore about your kitchen. You always have such a well-stocked larder. I found this delightful little Sara Lee thing in your freezer."

"I could use some tea." What was he doing in the house?

"I slept in your bed last night. I hope you don't mind."

"As long as I wasn't in it." Was that glib enough?

"You're so old-fashioned about that. How many times have I told you? I kept hoping you'd come home and wake me with some sort of pleasant surprise. I waited and waited for you last night and finally fell asleep."

"I'll change the sheets after you leave," she said.

He sloshed the hot water into the china teapot and took another china cup and saucer from the glass-doored cupboard. The matching cream and sugar dishes were on the table along with the pastry ring, also on a matching plate. Was he always this elaborate when he had a cup of tea by himself? "Will you have your usual, my dear?"

"Please." She'd soon know what her usual was. Did Diane really ever drink tea?

She sat down as he poured. He dropped two heaping teaspoons of sugar into the tea, then a heavy splash of cream. Having handed her the cup and saucer, he prepared his own, sweetening and creaming more moderately. She thought him a charming hostess as she watched him delicately serve the pastry.

He nibbled and sipped in silence for a moment. Then he looked at her, his expression, suddenly intense and penetrating, quite different from what it had been up to that moment. "Why haven't you delivered the elephant to Bertini?"

She stared at him.

"You've gotten the money. Grant has given you the elephant. Why haven't you split with Grant and given the thing to Bertini? He's getting a bit restless."

"I'll take care of everything soon enough."

"You're dealing with serious businessmen. Time is money. Don't play games with them. I came here last night to encourage you to finish what you've started so beautifully."

"Please let me handle it."

"I hope you're not developing nerves. You did a nice bit of work leading Grant down the garden path. Everyone is pleased with you. The only risk involved at this point would come from holding things up. Why spoil a good job?"

"I'll handle it in my own way soon enough."

He studied her for a moment, staring and then squinting, as if trying to decide if she was up to something. Then he dropped his eyes to his plate and toyed with the cake and drank his tea. After touching the linen napkin to his lips, he stood up and walked away from the table. She remained seated, her arms folded, waiting to see what he would do next.

He returned wearing his jacket. "Bertini will be calling you. May I suggest that you invite him to come by and pick the thing up?"

"What if I choose to return the money instead?"

"Don't be a bloody fool." He turned and left.

She reached out and grabbed Diane's handbag. The thin brown envelope was sealed with transparent tape. She could surely find more and reseal it. The envelope contained a single drawing, perhaps seventeen inches by twenty-four; detailed electronic circuitry, lines, symbols and numbers. In the lower right hand corner was a nameplate: Penn-Harrington Electronics. The elephant?

The phone rang, and after a moment's hesitation, she followed the sound into the next room. She'd have to start answering phone calls sooner or later. She picked it up.

"Diane."

"Yes."

"Diane, this is John Hodgeson. I'm afraid I have bad news for you."

She listened without comment as he re-created her accident on the way home from a week away in the Poconos . . .

"I'll get there as quickly as I can, Mr. Hodgeson." Her voice cracked. "Thank you so much for handling everything."

"The funeral has been set for Monday. I'll see if I can't have the necessary legal paperwork prepared by Tuesday at the latest. You'll probably want to get back to the Coast as soon as you can."

"Yes, I will."

She listened to his gracefully phrased condolences and told him that she, too, wished they were to be seeing each other under more pleasant circumstances, finally getting him off the phone. Then she broke into tears. The phone rang again; she stopped crying but didn't pick up the receiver. Once it was quiet she dialed information and then TWA, reserving a seat on a Sunday morning flight to JFK.

She got up and wandered through the house. Upstairs she found Diane's bedroom, the unmade canopied fourposter and an adjoining bath. She turned on the hot water in the tub, and returned to the bedroom, where she peeled off her clothes, leaving them on the floor where they fell. Diane's way, not hers. As she lowered herself into the totally enveloping therapy of the hot bath, the phone rang again, twelve rings before stopping. It rang again during the half hour she spent in the tub. She counted sixteen rings.

Submerged to her chin in the tub she kept steamy with a steady trickle of hot water, she felt the pain, which had been a continuous preoccupation since the night before, dissolving and flowing out of her body. Then she felt drained, almost without physical strength. Sleep. The only thing she could think about was sleep. The massive bed, already opened, invited her to withdraw, to hide from the world until her strength returned.

The phone rang again. She pulled herself from the tub, grabbed a towel, and answered it. "Hello."

"This's Bertini. I'm ready to pick up the elephant."

Hadn't the Englishman said Bertini knew she had it? She had to try and put him off. "I need a little more time."

"What's a little more time? Half an hour?"

"Middle of next week."

"Middle of the week? You outa your goddamn head? You got your money. I gotta have the elephant or things are going to get messy."

She should give it to him and get it over with. But that would be perpetuating the whole illegal business. She needed time to sort things out. "Please," she said. "Please give me a little longer. I don't have it."

"Well. You don't sound so smart-ass for a change. What happened to you?"

"I just need more time. That's all." He must have picked up the terror she felt.

"I thought you already had the thing. What's going on?"

Was he then in doubt about whether or not she had it? She wasn't up to meeting another stranger. "I've got to have until the middle of the week."

"Too long. Everybody's waiting. Waiting time costs money. Get it quicker."

She had convinced him. She held her breath for a moment. "Call me Thursday."

"Listen, I gotta tell you something. There's a couple people, including like Crease for instance, got the impression you're stalling. Whatever the hell you're up to, do yourself a goddamn favor. Have it Monday."

"I've got to fly East for a couple of days. Call me Wednesday."

"Didn't you just get back from somewhere? You ain't been home. I been ringing your goddamn phone off the wall."

"Did you call twice during the last half hour?"

"Once. Why didn't you answer?"

"I was taking a bath." Someone else had also called.

"I'm calling you Monday. You better be back and have it by then."

"Wednesday. Please. Goodbye."

She hung up, then got under the covers. The pillow was faintly scented; aftershave or cologne, she thought. She reversed the pillow, took the phone off the hook, and rolled over on her stomach.

What was the Englishman's name? Did he come and go as he pleased? Was Bertini the button man who was threatening to act like a button man? Who was Crease? She was too tired for the moment to be frightened. Sleep came, mercifully, before she could ask herself one more unanswerable question.

4

Her small circle of friends had really cared about her. She studied their faces, some puffy with tears of grief, as they filed by her, the only surviving relative, touching her, expressing sympathy, then taking their seats on the hard chairs in the little room of the funeral home, an open casket in front of them, an exact likeness of her on display inside it.

She wept openly. For Diane. And for all the people in the room that she was giving up in favor of the group Diane referred to as "creeps and misfits." For Roger, standing alone, his handsome face tight with the agony of losing her. Roger, it's all right. I'm me. That's Diane. Yes, Roger. Of course I'll marry you.

She wept for Angela, the friendly little dynamo who made the *Reporter Dispatch* her life. Angela, it's all right. I'll be into the office in a few days after all this is over and help you get caught up with everything.

And she wept for all the others, not a very glamorous crowd, hardly a crowd, in fact, but more, much more, than she wanted to give up. She had made a mistake, a terrible mistake, a stupid mistake. She wept for her stupidity. Listen, everybody! Listen. Don't be taken in by this little session of black humor. That's my twin sister, Diane, in the casket. Some of you remember Diane. Right? *She* was the one who was killed by the fog and the curve and the deer and the headlights and the sports car in the other lane. I walked away from it. Please recognize me. My hair's tied back, but it's me—please stop me from doing what I'm doing!

She listened to the eulogy, delivered so touchingly by Larry Patterson, his voice warm with feeling when he described how young and beautiful and full of life and wonderful to everyone she had been. She was listening to her own eulogy! How many people have experienced that? And she wept as she listened. She hadn't been all that wonderful to everyone. She could do much better. How many people ever had the opportunity to leave and come back and say that?

And she wept painfully at the cemetery as she watched them lower the casket. Oh, Diane!

It was finally over, and she could return to the house, her home, her family's home all her life, to be hers only two more days, days made ugly by the masquerade she would have to keep up.

"You're so like Ann, it's remarkable."

"People always said they could hardly tell us apart."

"We're going to miss her. I just don't know how we'll get along without her."

"I'm sorry I didn't see her more myself these last few years."

The Tuesday session with little Mr. John Hodgeson was somber, but businesslike as usual.

"You really should read all those things before you sign them."

"You've told me what's in them. I feel completely secure when matters like these are in your hands. My father thought so highly of you."

"Thank you, my dear. You can count on me to take care of everything. I'll use my own judgment in disposing of things. We'll all miss your sister terribly around here."

Her hand trembled as she took the pen. She started writing and stopped, then managed somehow to make a "Di" out of the "An," remembering Diane's angular signature as she formed the letters.

"Very good, my dear. And now, this one for Ann's life insurance."

She signed. "Thank you for everything, Mr. Hodgeson."

"Do you think you'd consider coming back here to live?"

Yes. Yes, of course. "No, I guess not. I'm afraid I've become a San Franciscan."

"The district attorney's office."

"I'd like to speak to him, please."

"Could you tell me who's calling?"

"I really don't think it's necessary. I only want to ask him a question."

"Couldn't you call your own attorney?"

"I'd really like to get my question answered by someone on the, well, the prosecuting side rather than the defense side of the issue."

"May I ask what this is all about? The district attorney is really quite busy."

"Well, I'm writing a book about twin sisters and there's a question of legalities involved when—"

"Just a moment, please."

"The delay seemed interminable. Finally, "Chavez." A man's voice, slight accent.

"Is this the district attorney?"

"I'm one of his assistants. May I help you?"

"I'd appreciate it. I'm writing a novel about twin sisters who are involved in an auto accident and one is . . . one doesn't survive the accident, and the other decides to assume the life of the dead sister and pretend she was killed instead of her sister."

"Sounds interesting. What's the problem?"

"Well, what I want to know is, is she breaking any law by doing this?"

"What kind of law?"

"I don't know. Fraud, or something like that."

"Who would she be defrauding?"

"Well, she'd be inheriting her own estate as though she were her sister. And assuming her dead sister's estate, as well."

"Is she her sister's beneficiary?"

"Well, yes, as far as I know."

"As far as you know? Aren't you writing the book?"

"Yes, of course. What I mean is, I hadn't thought about that. But let's say she is the beneficiary of her sister's estate, then does that mean she hasn't broken any law?"

"I can't think of one. Both estates are legally hers, regardless of the name she assumes. You can't be guilty of fraud against yourself."

"That's good to hear."

"On second thought, there is one angle where she could get into a real mess if she got caught."

"There is?"

"Sure. Insurance. If she signs her sister's name and collects her own insurance, then she's in it up to her neck. Jesus, I'd love to get my teeth into a case like that. It'd be a waltz. She's guilty of forgery with intent to defraud a third party. Obtaining money under false pretenses. And the payment could be double indemnity besides. You just don't collect your own life insurance."

"I see," she said softly. "What if she declines to accept payment of the insurance?"

"How would she explain doing a thing like that? People like having money handed to them."

"That's a good point." She wondered why she'd bothered to ask since she had already signed to receive the money. She remembered feeling when she bought the policy that it wasn't necessary. But Roger had talked her into it. Buy it at an early insurance age and have it for the time when you'll need it.

"Well, that take care of your questions?"

"Yes. I think so."

"Good. I'll have to watch for your book. Better still, send me a copy. I get a kick out of reading mysteries. What's your name?"

"My name? Ann Lombard."

"I'll remember it. Thought of a title?"

"Not yet."

"Well, Miss Lombard, glad to be of help."

"I really appreciate it."

"Don't thank me, just send me a copy when it comes out. Mario Chavez, care of the D.A.'s office."

"I won't forget."

She put the phone down and suddenly began to tremble. Why had she said Ann? And then Lombard? Why couldn't she have said Smith, or Jones, or Bertini. Suppose he read about the accident and was intrigued and started digging into the case? She could end up with as much trouble on the East Coast as she had in San Francisco.

The hardest part of Tuesday night was continuing the masquerade with Roger, who was unrelenting in his search for likenesses of Ann to cling to in those final moments. When she mentioned her plans to fly back the next morning, he offered to take her to the airport. She refused, but agreed to let him drive her to White Plains, where she could take a limousine.

When he arrived Wednesday morning she walked out of the house without looking back. She carried a small suitcase, one that matched those which had been found in the trunk of the car. As she said goodbye, she sensed that he wanted very much to fall in love with Diane, the ultimate Ann surrogate. When he kissed her on the cheek, she had to force herself to resist turning her face to his.

After a tedious limousine ride to the airport, she checked in and started for the gate. Entering the long tunnel to the boarding area, she was suddenly frightened. She stopped before she reached the middle and leaned against the tubular wall, trembling, looking away from the people who stared at her as they walked by in both directions.

Finally, she walked on. As she reached the highest point in the middle of the tunnel and started downhill, her stride became confident. Her right hand gripped the bag with the shoulder strap. The two brown envelopes were still in it.

The plane broke through the slight overcast and into the sunlight. She felt clear-eyed, done with crying, tuned to what was ahead. Ann was dead, dead and buried.

Diane lived.

5

She turned the key in the lock for the second time in seventy-two hours. She was, it seemed, irrevocably committed. "Up to her neck," as Chavez had put it. And the idea of getting caught, the cheap sensationalism, the embarrassment, even prison—these were impossible to comprehend for someone who had never gotten a parking ticket! This thought led to a remarkably singular and resolute conclusion: Diane must live. And without making any stupid mistakes.

There was so much to know, so much to learn. She entered the house and began exploring it, area by area, studying Diane by studying her house in an organized, methodical, Ann way. The top floor of the house contained three bedrooms—a guest room, a studio bedroom, and Diane's bedroom with its dressing area and bath. A second bath opened off the hall. An elegant living-dining room dominated the middle level, which also included the front entrance, the kitchen and breakfast area, a library-bar, and a small powder room. The lower floor provided another bedroom, rather plainly furnished as if for a servant's quarters, a utility area, and a garage containing a bright-yellow foreign car, an Alfa Romeo. She found she loved Diane's taste throughout the place, without reservation.

She spent over two hours in Diane's dressing area, going over her wardrobe, cosmetics, and perfumes. She enjoyed moving from drawer to closet to drawer, trying on pants suits and long skirts, wondering whether she would really be comfortable discarding her shirtwaist dresses and tailored slacks for such attention-getting clothes. It was going to be fun to try.

In the kitchen-dining area she examined dishes, silver, glassware, and food supplies, memorizing their locations. The bar in the library was well stocked, and she found back-up supplies, heavy on vodka, in the utility room. There was also a large wine rack nearly filled with French, Portuguese, and California wines.

The desk in the library was the business center of Diane's empire. By examining the bills and the checkbook, she got a feel for her sister's shopping and spending patterns, all rather free. She found Diane's signature and practiced duplicating it. And there was correspondence, presenting a few more names for her to remember. The more she studied, the more convinced she became that she was trying to do something virtually impossible. Only the fact that the alternatives to trying seemed more complicated and even less appealing kept her at it.

Realizing that she knew nothing about her adopted city, she left the house and went for a walk, .hiking to the nearest service station for a map. She also bought copies of all the city's newspapers. The walk up and down the steep hills left her leg muscles tied in knots. Once back inside the house, she spread out the map and studied it carefully. She then leafed through the newspapers, checking for style and features, but concentrating on advertisements, noting major stores and locating them on the map.

She gradually began to feel the choking sensation of panic. She had been a fool, a complete fool! No matter how bright, how organized, how quick she was, it all added up to something that couldn't be done without slipping up somewhere.

The sound of the telephone ringing increased her panic, but she picked up the receiver after two rings. "Hello."

"Diane? It's John Sturdi. We met on the plane Saturday morning."

"Hello." Glad to hear from you, mister, because you're a godsend—the one person in San Francisco I know who didn't know Diane.

"I called to see if you'd like to get together for a drink, and maybe dinner."

"I'd love it. When?"

"This evening? I know it's short notice."

"No problem."

"Can you meet me at eight-thirty at Ernie's?"

"I'll be there."

Ernie's. Hopefully, there would be only one. She

turned to the yellow pages, noted the address, and located it on the map. Then she looked at her watch. Almost seven o'clock. Time to get ready for her first date in San Francisco.

After a delicious meal followed by one drink at a colorful bar that was a favorite of Sturdi's, they were back at the house. She opened the door with some trepidation—would the pink Englishman be there? No sign of anyone.

As Sturdi was mixing drinks, the phone rang. She looked at her watch and answered it.

"You're back!"

"Apparently." Who was he?

"How were things on the East Coast? How's your twin?"

"Fine." She shuddered.

"Glad to hear it. I figured I'd give you a call and see if you were home."

"At one A.M.?" She glanced at Sturdi.

"Come on, I've never known you to go to bed this early. Besides, I called earlier and no answer. When'd you get back?"

"Yesterday. Late." Whoever he was, she liked the way he sounded.

"Why didn't you call me?"

"Kind of out of it from the trip."

"So it seems. You don't sound like yourself. Have you heard from Bertini?"

"Yes. Saturday."

"Saturday? You were in New York Saturday."

"What am I thinking about? This coast-to-coast travel has my brain scrambled. Friday."

"Friday? You didn't mention it when you called me from the airport. Diane? Is that you? Are you all right?"

"It's me and I'm fine, only tired. The pace has been too much even for me." She glanced at Sturdi again. "I was up earlier than usual this morning." Diane must have lived totally as a night person.

"Did you give Bertini the elephant?"

"Not yet."

"Why not?"

"I don't know."

"I thought it was you who was supposed to corrupt me. Have you got our money?"

Our money? This, then, was Beecher Grant. Had to be. "Yes, I have it."

"Then give him the thing. That was the deal, and we'll have trouble if we don't. And let's get together tomorrow and divvy up and celebrate."

"Sounds great. When tomorrow?"

"You sound funny."

"I don't think my head's on straight at the moment." A good Diane line.

"Why don't I come over around seven?"

"Seven's fine." Sturdi looked disappointed.

"You going to have Victoria feed us?"

"I don't know. What do you think?" Who was Victoria?

"What the hell. Since we're celebrating, let's drive over to Kirby's. He'll fix us something special."

"I'll skip lunch."

"That's my Diane. Tomorrow at seven. You know, I haven't seen you in a while."

"We can catch up tomorrow night. See you then." She looked at Sturdi. "Sorry I took so long," she said, automatically, preoccupied with the notion of a creature named Victoria who fed Diane and her boy friends.

He set his empty glass down. "When can I see you again? Obviously not tomorrow night."

"Call me in a couple of days—you're probably busier than I am. Which reminds me. You mentioned during dinner that you were involved in some way in electronics. What would the word 'elephant' mean to someone in electronics?"

Too quickly, he met her question with a question. "What do you know about an elephant?"

Impossible. She'd met him on an airplane! "I don't know anything about it," she said.

"Then why did you mention it?"

"Just curious. I just happened to hear a conversation that struck me as peculiar. Two men talking about an elephant as though it was something electronic."

He studied her, trying to gauge the truth in her story. "Your friend on the phone just now, maybe?"

"No, no, it wasn't him." Suddenly, unreasonably, she felt convinced that Sturdi knew Beecher Grant and may have casually known Diane. "I really don't remember who it was," she went on. "I didn't pay that much attention."

"Funny thing to have overheard," he said.

"Is it something unusual?"

"Possibly." He paused. "I'd better be getting along. It's been great but I've got work tomorrow."

"I've enjoyed it too, John. I can't tell you how much."

He stood up. "Let me know if you hear anything more about an elephant." His tone was a little edgy. Then, in an easier tone, "I'll call in a couple of days."

She closed the door behind him and went into the library. What would be on television at that hour? She settled into an easy chair and began working the remote-control device. Maybe an old spy movie. As she thought of Bertini and Beecher Grant and the Englishman and her suspicious stranger-date who seemed to know more about the elephant than *she* did, it occurred to her that a spy movie might give her some training she could use.

The thought was not a comforting one.

Realizing that she was wide awake, despite the lateness of the hour, she got up and found her glass and poured herself a little more scotch. She was halfway through it before she realized that it was the first time in her life she had ever had a drink alone.

6

She reached out of her sleep for the phone. "Hello."

"It's Slick Bertini and it's Thursday. Where the hell were you yesterday?"

"My God! What time is it?" Still half asleep, she found the voice painfully loud.

"Eight o'clock."

"Eight o'clock? Did you have to call so early?"

"Most people are working already. You got the elephant?"

"Yes."

He paused. "I'm coming to pick it up." His voice sounded lighter, somewhat relaxed.

"Fine. What time?"

"Whadda ya mean, what time? Now. I'm parked in front of your house."

"Have you got a phone in your car?"

"You know goddamn well I got a phone in my car."

I do now. "Fine. I'll bring it right down."

She put on a robe, took the thin brown envelope out of her handbag, and went to the front door. She opened it to find a stocky, coarse-featured man wearing ill-fitting clothes and an absurdly ferocious scowl. A prototype hood.

"Here's the envelope," she said.

"Why don't you invite me in? Do yourself a favor." He smiled, and she decided that she really preferred the scowl.

"Please. I've got to go back to bed."

"Like I said, invite me in."

"I thought you were in a big hurry to deliver this thing to all those people who are already at work."

"I got a few minutes. And like I told ya before, I'm a good friend to have."

"Please move your foot," she said. Would he move it?

He slid it back and the smile left his face. "This thing better be right."

"I don't know anything about it. This is what they gave me."

"If it's not right, I'll be back to see you."

"Please try to understand. All I can do is pass along what they give me."

As he turned and went back to the large car, she closed the door and twisted the deadlatch. Then she went back to bed. The elephant had been delivered.

She thought she heard the teakettle again. She rolled over and glanced at the little table clock. Twelve-thirty. The whistle persisted. Hadn't she turned the deadlatch when she shut the front door? She padded out into the hall. Definitely the teakettle..

After slipping something on, she went down to the breakfast area, her steps soundless on the thick carpeting, and when she appeared suddenly, he jumped. The table was spread with his usual proper array of cups, saucers, teapots, and pastry. "Don't you have any tea bags at your house?" she asked.

"You gave me a bit of a start." He took a sip of tea. "I was expecting you to show up, but you still managed to creep up on me. Rather like an American Indian. Care for some tea?"

She was beginning to like him a little, to find a kind of warmth behind his fussy manner. "You know I can't stand tea," she said, smiling.

"Nonsense. You adore tea."

"Then fix me my usual. Incidentally, I thought I latched the door."

"The front door." He made up her cup of tea, heavy with milk and sugar. "There you are."

She sat down and tasted it, wondering, as before, whether Diane had really liked the bland, sweet concoction.

"Every time I've tried to call you the past few days, you've been out."

"I'm surprised you weren't over here checking up on me."

"I guess I really do find it hard staying away from the old place. As a matter of fact, I have come by a time or two. You do run around."

"It's the only way to fly." Diane lines were coming more easily.

"Where's Victoria? On holiday? I haven't seen her around."

Victoria again. She wondered if her hired help lived in. The bedroom in the basement? "She wanted a few days off."

His expression changed. "Have you delivered the elephant?"

"Yes."

He exhaled with great relief. "Very good. Have you paid off Grant?"

"Tonight."

"Very good. Very, very good." A happy grin. "I am truly pleased to hear it. Now I can collect mine. Here, let me heat up your tea." He poured a little more into her cup.

"You seem pleased," she said.

"Shouldn't I be? I assured them you could handle it, you know. I told them you could be counted on. Very nice. The money's very nice, isn't it? Very green."

She smiled. "Extremely green."

He finished his tea and stood up. "I think I'll hurry on. Do have a pleasant evening. See you tomorrow night."

He left her smiling. Diane must have liked him more than she'd indicated. But what was his name and what was happening the next night? She had latched the front door. Where did he come in and why did he feel so free in the house? He called it "the old place." What was his role in the whole business?

And Victoria? She rushed downstairs to the bedroom on the lower level. The drawers were full of clothes—uniforms, underwear, stockings. The small bathroom contained a few toiletries. She pulled a uniform from a drawer and held it up. Beige with a white collar and cuffs. Victoria. What was she like? And how, she wondered, did Diane get along with her?

Since the best way to learn a city is to drive in it, she got dressed and went down to the garage. The overhead door was open; the Englishman must have come in that way. The door from the garage into the house also had a deadlatch, something else to remember.

After finding the right key and studying the controls of the little car, she started it, backed out into the street, and headed it down hill. She'd have to adapt to San Francisco driving and a foreign car at the same time. With the city map on the seat beside her, the several hours' drive was an exhilarating adventure of starts, stalls, whining gears, near-misses, and screaming horns. She drove up and down the hills, seeing many things in daylight that she had seen with Sturdi the night before. Streets, places, and things seemed slightly familiar. She was getting there.

She got back to the house and spent a leisurely hour selecting a delectable pants suit to wear to dinner. Becoming accustomed to Diane's wardrobe would be one of the pleasanter aspects of the game.

Makeup, on the other hand, wouldn't be so easy. She had never used much, and Diane had gone for dramatic eye effects. After several abortive attempts at two-tone shadow and an outright confession of defeat to a set of false eyelashes, her eyes seemed acceptable if not great.

As she was admiring the effect of vaguely mauve eyelids, the telephone rang.

61

"It's me, mum. You told me to call in a week."
Another English accent. "Have you been back long?"

"No, not long." So Victoria was British.

"Would you like me to come back tonight? Are you having dinner in?"

"No, it's not necessary. I'm going out to dinner. But do come tomorrow."

"Yes, mum. Is everything all right? How was your sister?"

"She was fine."

"Did you tell her about it?"

She hesitated, wondering if Diane told Victoria everything. Then, "I sure did."

"What did she think you should do?"

"Let's talk about it tomorrow, and I'll bring you up to date." I need a friend and you're elected.

"Very good, mum. Tomorrow."

She hung up, feeling lighthearted, almost happy, for the first time in San Francisco. She liked the Englishman. She was going to like Victoria. And in thirty minutes she would meet the man Diane had been starting to like "a little too much." He would be gorgeous, and fun, and greatly admiring of mauve eyelids and soft blue pants suits, and—

Oh, God . . . What would she have to do now to keep the game going?

7

He *was* gorgeous! Tall, deeply tanned, his blond curly hair longer than Roger's. He stood smiling, expectant, his eyes warm though startlingly blue.

When he took her head in his hands, she stood and let it happen. She felt his mouth on hers, then on her neck. His hands slid down and around her. She put hers around him, feeling awkward as she tried to relax.

"The next time your sister issues a summons," he said, his mouth somewhere near her ear, "don't stay so long."

"Mmm, think how nice it is getting back."

"What did she want with you, anyway?"

"Family stuff. Boring but essential." Diane always found most things boring.

"Why don't you fix us a drink?"

His mouth was on her neck again. It had never occurred to her that her neck was so sensitive. "It'll be a little difficult under the circumstances."

"Then let it wait." He kissed her again, a lingering kiss that left her lightheaded. Then he released her. "Why don't you fix us a drink?"

She turned toward the library. What did he drink? What did Diane drink? "You fix the drinks," she said.

"Since when?"

"Since now."

He walked into the library and looked into the ice bucket. "You don't even have any ice out."

A lesson learned. Ice in the ice bucket. "I thought we might be going straight out tonight."

"You're kidding. Tonight? Let's mix some drinks and make a big pile of money on the floor and sit in the middle of it and play with it and get bombed out of our skulls."

"Sounds like a good party. I'll get some ice."

"And the money!"

She went into the kitchen and pulled an ice tray. After dumping it into the bucket, she watched him drop some into a glass pitcher and add lots of vodka and very little vermouth. That explained the heavy vodka supply downstairs. She'd have to learn to drink vodka martinis, dry, and like them. She watched him select two heavy-bottomed tumblers off the shelf under the bar. Hardly martini glasses. She'd know next time.

Going to her bag, she drew out the fat brown envelope and tossed it at him. "What do you make of these?"

He dumped the ten packets out on the floor. "They

64

make such nice, tight bundles when they're new, don't they? Did you notice the lovely little green noise they made when they hit the ground?" He poured the drinks, transferring a couple of ice cubes to each glass, and handed her one. Then he dropped to the floor and began examining one of the packets. "I hope we don't get our tail feathers singed over these."

"You mean we might?"

"Is it really possible to get something like this for nothing?"

She took a swallow of the biggest drink she'd ever held in her hand and almost gagged. A long, long way from the diluted scotch she was used to.

As they talked, she sat on the floor and sipped cautiously, a tiny swallow at a time; still, the level of the drink was going down.

His drink was going faster than hers. Did Diane keep up? She took a slightly larger sip. He said something about the money, and as she replied, she pronounced the words carefully.

He got up and fixed two more drinks, draining the melted ice from the pitcher into the ice bucket before adding the liquor. Why dilute good drinks?

As he returned to the floor and refilled their glasses, she shuddered at the thought of more vodka. Her head was beginning to swim. How much of this stuff did Diane drink? A lot. Diane was a drinker. And they were celebrating the pile of money on the floor. She took a sip of the drink. It was beginning to taste better—a clean, cold taste, not at all like polish remover.

She wondered when they would leave to go to dinner. She'd have to eat soon. Her head felt loose. When she tried to talk, the words came out mushy, and this made her giggle. She found she was giggling a great deal for no reason. She watched him take another swallow and so she took another. Her head threatened to topple over. She felt it going and moved to get back under it, giggling as she did. It happened again, and she dove under it again.

Suddenly, she noticed that his expression had changed. He was studying her and smiling a funny, new smile. She dipped toward him to catch her head and then pulled back, almost falling over backward, giggling. Why was he looking at her that way?

He moved forward on his knees and kissed her. "I've got an idea," he said.

She tried to speak the word "What?" and wondered what it sounded like.

He picked up a packet of hundred-dollar bills, broke the paper band, and scattered the bills on the floor. Then another bunch, and another, and another.

She asked a question, hoping it would come out as, "What the hell do you think you're doing?"

"We're going to make this a night to remember," he said. "We're going to consecrate this beautiful money."

Without taking his eyes off her, he began loosening his tie.

She fumbled with the little ascot at her neck.

He yanked his tie off and threw it on the floor, sending the jacket after it. He began unbuttoning his shirt.

She tried, "When are we going to have dinner?"

"Later." He extended his hand to help her to her feet. Then he began unbuttoning his shirt again.

She tried the buttons on the pants-suit top, her fingers incredibly clumsy. One by one, she finally fumbled

66

her way to the waist. She reached for the zipper on the pants; it seemed to have disappeared. She stood weaving, looking at him, and began to giggle. What would Diane do? Surely she wouldn't just stand there and giggle.

Piece by piece, her clothes seemed to dissolve away. The bikini panties were the toughest. She almost fell as she wrestled them off her feet. That finished it. Nothing left. Diane must live.

She lowered herself to her knees on the green paper. Sorry, Roger. You're no longer the only one since Charlie. Good old Charlie from Harvard Yard.

Beecher's hands felt cool, but his body was warm and his lips were warm. She thought briefly of her cluttered desk at the *Reporter Dispatch*.

Diane lives—on a mountain of green!

8

She remembered getting dressed again and walking out of the house with him, leaving the money all over the library floor. And she remembered his saying something about their giving the money a new wrinkle or two. And she remembered going in his car for a long drive, over the Golden Gate Bridge and then over back roads to a small houselike structure on the edge of a lot of water. Far across that water she saw what must have been the lights of San Francisco. And somewhere in front of the house was a sign: "The Caprice."

She recalled the interior as cozy and charming. And someone named Kirby, who looked like a youngish Ernest Hemingway, came to their table to chat and then ordered for them. The food, which was wonderful, began to take some of the swim out of her head. But Kirby, in his chef's hat, appeared with a bottle of wine, and soon her head was reeling again as she ate, becoming full, very full, sluggish and leaden.

She remembered driving home with him, almost asleep and almost sick, the ride endless. And she recalled a sip of Drambuie ("Okay, a quick nightcap." "What's with you? Can't you hold it any more?"), then standing in the middle of the scattered money as if it weren't there, wanting only to slip into that huge fourposter to die awhile and try and recover her sense of normalcy. And she remembered being lifted by him, carried up the stairs and eased down onto the bed and left there, still fully clothed, only to have the entire room begin to bob and sway, almost float, and finally go spiraling off into blackness.

She stared up at the canopy over her head. The bed was still rocking on water. A little daylight penetrated the draperies, and she rolled over onto one side to look at the clock: not quite eight. On the table next to the clock was a packet of bills, held together neatly by a rubber band. She rolled back and closed her eyes to wait for the room to settle down. Sleep. More sleep.

The sound of the door to the room startled her, and she opened her eyes again. She looked up at someone standing next to the bed, someone seventy-five stories high, wearing a beige dress trimmed in white, someone with a huge, milk-white face and gray hair, grinning at her, the face distorted by the grin and by the angle from which she saw the grin. The face was all teeth and nostrils.

She looked with one eye at the specter by the bed. How could it smile? "Later," she said finally. "Later. Let me sleep some more. Got to sleep some more." She pulled the sheet over her face.

She opened her eyes and studied the canopy again. What time this time? Both hands straight up. Twelve noon. The sunlight glinted through the slit that separated the drapes. Her head throbbed as if creased down the middle. Creased. Crease. Who was Crease? She lay still, concentrating on the texture of the cloth above her, following thread lines as far as she could without moving her head. It hurt too much to move.

The woman in the beige uniform was back, carrying a fizzy glass. "Here you are, mum."

Having made it to a sitting position, she huddled on the edge of the bed beneath the crushing weight of her swollen head, then took the glass and drank it down. Victoria was tall, very tall, big-boned and gawky, with a beaked nose and slightly protruding teeth. Her smile was open and engaging.

"From the looks of things," Victoria said, "I'd say you had yourself quite a few last night."

"I wish I knew how many," she said, "so I'd know how many not to have next time." She returned the glass and stood up to struggle with zippers and buttons. She'd gotten the pants suit off once and back on again the night before, hadn't she?

"Do you think you'll be able to eat any breakfast mum?"

"Coffee. Lots of black coffee."

Victoria left, and she stepped out of the puddle of clothes on the floor and went into the bathroom. This time she used the shower, standing for a long time with the water streaming down her head, neck and body. Better. Her head was much better.

She put on the robe and went down to the kitchen. "Victoria?"

"Yes, mum?"

"Victoria, what's your last name?"

"Come along, now. Why would you be asking that? You know it as well as your own."

"If I knew it, I wouldn't ask."

"Oh, what are you up to now?"

"Sit down, Victoria. I've something interesting to tell you."

9

At first Victoria was disbelieving, then stunned, and, finally, grief-stricken.

She watched in morbid fascination as Victoria's big face registered shock after shock. Victoria, who had obviously adored Diane with a dedication that was almost worship, came around slowly to a resigned acceptance of the facts. Accidents happen, and Diane was gone forever. And a new Diane had appeared to take the place of the one departed, a new one so like the old one that people would never know the difference.

It came as no surprise that Victoria had always been fascinated by Diane's frantically paced life-style, or that Victoria had found Diane's hanky-panky during recent months dangerous, more than just fascinating. It was high adventure, an adventure so rife with excitement and intrigue, she said, she would have worked for Diane for nothing just to be in on it.

"I was her chief of staff," Victoria explained. As, in fact, she must have been. She had covered for Diane, provided alibis, and, most important, helped develop strategies to meet the problems that arose. And obviously Diane had found Victoria an aide-de-camp of incalculable value.

She could also sense that Victoria was aware of the impact and significance of this latest development, and was already warming to the prospect of new complications.

They spent the entire day sitting at the breakfast table, sipping coffee and talking, reviewing, scheming, evaluating. A new alliance had been formed, one which was potentially stronger than that which had preceded it.

Victoria had the answers to many of the troublesome questions. The pink Englishman's name was Henry Mapleway. He had previously owned Diane's house and had sold it because he needed the money. He seemed to earn his living by gambling. He retained keys to the house and came and went at odd times, almost like a close relative, or a boarder. Mapleway had approached Diane on the spy thing, and when Diane had become sufficiently fascinated by the notion and by the prospect of all the money, he'd introduced her to Beecher Grant who worked at Penn-Harrington, where something called an elephant had been developed.

"Victoria, just what is the elephant?"

"Oh, I don't know, luv. Some sort of electronic marvel."

Big help. "Go on."

Diane's job had been to get to know Beecher and convince him to get details on the elephant. Beecher hadn't taken much convincing. The two of them were to pass this information on to Bertini, who was a contact for another company, Peninsula Micronics. He had delivered the money in advance as an inducement not to lose their nerve, and a hundred thousand dollars is a substantial inducement. The money was there because Peninsula Micronics had been acquired by the Syndicate as a "legitimate" investment, and the Syndicate was anxious to see that the investment proved profitable.

"Victoria, all of this is very, very illegal, Why is Diane doing it?"

"Because, luv, Diane needs the money. And because Diane is too afraid of the consequences to turn back. That's why Diane must fly to her wise sister for advice."

Her wise sister. "What if Diane doesn't need the money any more?"

"But she's all finished with that part of it." Victoria paused and thought a moment. "Don't you see? Now you can stop worrying so much and devote yourself to playing the part of your sister."

Victoria was right. Turning back now would blow the game. There was no going back to being Ann the reporter—and, for Diane, the scary part was over; the elephant had been delivered and the money collected and divided. They were finished with it . . . weren't they? Then why had Beecher expressed concern?

"Okay, Victoria, if that's all finished, what is Diane doing next?"

"I think tonight she's going to a party." She went into the library and checked an appointment calendar on the desk. "Yes," she said, "she's going to a most unusual party."

"Who with?"

"Why, Mr. Mapleway. It's being given by some of his friends. Odd sorts, to say the least. Theatrical types and artists, I should think."

"And what should I expect there?"

"Drugs, among other things."

"Do I use any of them?"

"Only grass."

"Grass? You mean marijuana?"

"Pot, luv. Tea."

"And do I like it?"

"You absolutely adore it. Haven't you discovered your own supply?"

"No."

"The black velvet purse in your left-hand vanity drawer."

"I noticed it but didn't open it. I've never even seen the stuff before."

"Then perhaps we'd better give you a quick training program."

They went upstairs to the bedroom and took out the black handbag, which held a brass pipe and several small plastic bags containing crushed leaves. Victoria filled the pipe and lit it, took a deep drag, and handed it over. She had never smoked anything. With Victoria's encouragement, she finally puffed and inhaled, then coughed. Nothing. The smell was distasteful, slightly reminiscent of her five A.M. ride into New York a week before. She tried more, inhaling and holding her breath as Victoria coached her. Still nothing. What was all the fuss about grass? Victoria encouraged her on, explaining the ritual of taking a drag, inhaling deeply and holding as long as possible, passing the "stick" or the pipe on to the next person.

She took another drag, coughed and lost it, then tried still another. Her throat felt dry and the top of her scalp seemed to be tightening. Was this the forbidden pleasure? Victoria assured her it could get better, much better. And Victoria, who had been sharing the pipe, had a new relaxed look to her pleasant toothy smile.

They emptied the ash into the toilet and discussed what she should wear. Victoria selected a soft, shiny little dress in bright green, with a halter top, and bright-green high-heeled sandals. The halter top meant no bra. She slipped the dress over her head, loving the feel of the material against her skin. She'd have to get over the self-consciousness of not wearing proper underwear.

"Tell me, Victoria, Will Diane know anyone there?"

"A few people, I would expect. In fact, some of them have probably been here. But you'll be able to muddle through. Listen for first names and be friendly. Everyone there will be flying their own plane." Victoria grinned broadly. "I'll go down and fix you a bite to eat, luv. You mustn't go on an empty stomach."

She applied herself to the array of makeup, experimenting this time with navy mascara and soft gold eye shadow. Before starting downstairs, she pulled three of the hundred-dollar bills out of the packet. When she reached the kitchen, she handed them to Victoria. "I don't know what I pay you," she said, "but take this for now. You never know when you'll need some mad money."

Victoria smiled. "Oh, thanks, mum. A lady does like to be prepared these days."

The phone rang and Victoria answered it. "She may

have left, but I'll check. Who's calling, please? Mr. John Sturdi?"

She took the receiver. "Hello."

"You've got to go to a party with me tomorrow night. And I won't take no for an answer."

"What kind of party?"

"A swell one. Some of my business associates, some interesting people. Are we on?"

She accepted without checking Diane's engagement calendar. Maybe she'd learn more about the elephant.

10

Mapleway arrived at eight, a masterpiece in shiny blue. The combined effect of the neo-Edwardian jacket and pants, the ruffle-fronted shirt stretched over his paunch, the fancy shoes, and his overlong blue-gray hair and florid complexion brought to mind Gainsborough's Blue Boy, arrived at middle age. All he needed was a hat with a plume.

They drove to the party in his battered but still peppy English import—a Morgan, she noted, restraining the impulse to ask questions about a car she was supposed to know as a friend.

They parked in front of a large but shabby house in another part of town, located, like most houses in

San Francisco, on a very steep hill. Inside, they found a large, exuberant crowd and very little light. She thought she smelled—yes, there it was—the aroma from her afternoon practice session.

But people were drinking, too. And folk rock music was pouring into the room at a deafening volume. She was waved at, kissed, even embraced. As her eyes adjusted to the poor lighting, she found she was in the middle of a human menagerie: guru types, at least one midget, drag queens, white girls wearing afros or beribboned pigtails, black girls wearing headbands.

Some of them seemed nervous, hyperenergized; others seemed ready to fall asleep. One beautiful girl with flowing blonde hair lay perfectly still and quiet, stretched out on a window seat, her arms folded on her chest as if prepared for burial, her face floodlit by a tiny wall fixture. What was *she* on? Across the room, a young man in jeans held out a handful of brightly colored tablets and capsules. A girl with very short hair selected one and swallowed it without drinking. In a corner of the room a half dozen people sat on the floor, cross-legged, a long-tubed water pipe in the center of their circle, smoking and passing the mouthpiece from one to the next.

Mapleway appeared with a drink and then left her again. She sipped; the drink was tall and cold and dark-colored and bitter as gall. A freaky young man wearing wire-rimmed glasses and a handlebar mustache walked up to her, slid his hand inside her halter, and began massaging her left breast.

Controlling the urge to react explosively, she wondered who he was and where he was with Diane. She turned aside, amazed at her own cool, and said in a relaxed voice, "Do I know you from somewhere?"

"If not, you should, because we've got a little something going."

"*You've* got a little something going. I don't happen to be in on it."

"You lose big," he snapped, then walked away.

In one corner she spotted Mapleway, having an animated discussion with a straight type. In another corner of the room a bearded man had the rapt attention of a large circle of followers. He sat on a table, barefoot, his legs crossed, his hands with the palms together in front of his shabby African shirt, which was open to the waist.

She was a long way from Mount Kisco.

As bitter as the drink had been, she had almost finished it and wished she had another. The taste was beginning to grow on her. A straight-looking young man in a tie and jacket, and apparently new to the scene, began making small talk. She assured him the surroundings were pretty routine.

"Lanigan!" A male voice called through a break in the music. He was clean-shaven and slightly effeminate, with shoulder-length hair, a black turtleneck, and white slacks. "Been looking for you, doll. We're refilling the hookah. He grabbed her hand. "Where's Pinky?"

The pink Englishman? Or someone else? "He's around somewhere." A safe enough answer.

As he led her back toward the water pipe they passed a pretty young girl with a wild afro who was sitting alone, sobbing quietly, tears rolling down her face. They reached the circle around the water pipe. Sleeping Beauty, stretched out nearby, slumbered on.

She sat down and glanced around at the others, immediately characterizing them in her mind as familiar types—Toulouse-Lautrec, Tallulah Bankhead, Rosie

Grier. Then there was the young man who had brought her into the circle, plus two others, whom she read as a freaky couple who had gone establishment but were holding on to what little they could of something past. Mapleway slipped in beside her and handed her a fresh drink.

Toulouse-Lautrec lit the pipe. The mouthpiece came to her; remembering her afternoon's training, she took a drag, inhaled, held it, and passed the pipe on to Mapleway. The smoke tasted as it had in the afternoon, only cooler. Around the circle and back to her. She took another drag on the pipe—a "toke," she now knew, thanks to Tallulah. The members of the group became quiet and serious about what they were doing. Toulouse-Lautrec finally declared the bowl to be all ash. He unscrewed it, emptied it, refilled it from an ornate humidor, and lit the pipe again.

While waiting, she took a sip of her drink. It seemed stronger than before, the flavor more pronounced. The pipe came to her and she took a long, deep puff. She was beginning to feel a little strange, wondering perhaps if she should refuse further rounds or fake her next drag. But the bowl glowed with each puff. The tube was back to her and she took a drag and, after another round, one more.

The total effect hit her with no real warning. Suddenly her head felt hollow, her body sodden and immobile. She thought about moving out of the circle but realized her body would not obey. The sensation was so totally new that she found herself wondering what else might have been in the pipe. Perhaps they had tricked her into sampling some terrible addictive drug! She looked at the others in the circle with distrust and, then, with terror. Even Mapleway. She glared at Toulouse-Lautrec. "What did you put in that thing?"

"What? That's the best stuff in town," he answered, with an unexpected Bronx accent. "It's the best you can get in the whole Bay Area. One pound cost me a bundle."

"It's good stuff, Lanigan," said the young man who had led her to the circle.

She concentrated on holding herself still and quiet for a moment. She had read about the paranoia that sometimes strikes beginning pot smokers. She had already smoked it. And after all, whatever was in the pipe, they smoked it, too. She'd have to control herself or she'd give the game away. Somehow, she'd survive.

When the pipe came around once more, she took a tiny puff. She passed it on, and as she watched, the group gradually quit smoking and began to fall back from the pipe.

She sat and stared around her, feeling almost paralyzed. The others in the circle sat quietly as well. Mapleway dropped back to his elbows and rolled over on one side. Tallulah began to make low-voiced, moaning comments about how good she felt. Others in the room appeared elongated and seemed to float as they walked, in a kind of slow motion. The music pounded and swirled, each number seeming to go on and on, endlessly. The pulsating light—what there was of it—began to give the room a startling three-dimensional depth. She took a sip of her drink, and its bitterness penetrated into all the recesses of her head, producing a kind of stinging delicious pain. She felt as if she could separate by taste all of the individual elements of the unknown liquor in her glass.

She pushed herself backward along the floor until

she could prop her back against the base of the window seat where Sleeping Beauty lay at rest. Mapleway lay on his side, Tallulah on her back, making conversation with herself. Rosie Grier slumped against a wall. The two ex-dropouts got up and walked away, as did Toulouse-Lautrec.

Hours, days, years went by as she sipped her drink, tasting each sip a hundred times, feeling her body respond to the rhythmic pressure of the music and illumination. She could actually separate the sound into individual instruments, as if only one at a time were playing.

She became faintly aware that something was nuzzling her right ear; she ignored it until the music stopped and the nuzzler gave her ear a little nip. She turned around—it was Sleeping Beauty, leaning down from her position on the window seat.

"I think you have me confused with someone else," she told her. "You must be looking for Freddie." She giggled as she spoke, feeling detached.

"Freddie who? I'm looking for *you*."

"Well, you've found me. Now go find Freddie."

"What would I want with Freddie?"

"Search me."

"So nice of you to offer. I'd love to."

"Stick to Freddie. He's nice." She moved away from the girl and started edging toward Mapleway.

"Freddie is an unmitigated ass," she heard the girl say. A moment later, the girl had returned to her Sleeping Beauty position.

As the music began again, she realized that she was hungry. She crawled along the floor to where Mapleway still lay motionless on his side and touched his shoulder. "Aren't you starved?"

"I never felt better."

"I'm absolutely famished."

"In a little while."

She put her head on the curve of his well-padded hip and relaxed to absorb the music. She glanced at Sleeping Beauty, who had returned to her trance. A series of hysterical feminine screams emanated from some other part of the house and she sat up. Seeing that no one else was reacting in any way, she put her head back down on Mapleway and returned to her communication with the light patterns and music. She liked what was happening. She felt as if she were floating, looking down on herself in the group, pleased with what she saw. Perhaps there had been a little Diane dormant in her all along.

Hours and hours went by. She spent the time thinking about food, sweet and sour and pungent and peppery and creamy and soft and chewy and buttery, all succulent and totally satisfying. Finally, she shook her arms and legs. "I want food!" she shouted. "Mapleway, get me something to eat."

He rolled over, and her head hit the carpet. "I guess I could do with a bit of something myself. Why don't we split?"

She sat up. "Let's go somewhere good. Somewhere zingy."

They got up and he started leading her toward the door.

"Don't we say good night and thanks to somebody?" she asked.

He looked at her as if she were deranged. "I've no clue as to who's in charge. Besides, why disturb them?"

No one seemed remotely interested in their leaving. They drove to the middle of Chinatown and walked

85

up a poorly lit stairway to a small dining room, where they had an absolute feast. She felt as if she'd never tasted Chinese food before. At one point during the meal she glanced at a wall clock. It was after midnight. The one-week anniversary of her rebirth as Diane. What more could the next week possibly bring?

When they got back to her house, Mapleway followed her in for a nightcap. "Why don't I stay the night?" he asked after they'd sat awhile with their drinks.

"You're a dear to ask, but—"

"One of these days you really will have to surprise me. These are modern times, you know. Our relationship should be based on total communication."

"It's the best offer I've had all night, Henry. I mean it."

He left and she turned the deadlatch on the door. Then she went down to make sure the garage entry door was also locked. As she was on her way back up to the living room, she heard Mapleway shouting to her from outside, agonized, desperate shouts. She looked through the small window in the door; two men were beating him a few feet from the doorway. One held his arms while the other, wearing gloves, was hammering fists into his helpless body and face.

Opening the door, she screamed at them to leave him alone. Mapleway looked up and reached out to her. The man throwing punches stopped and began moving in her direction. She slammed the door shut and latched it just as Victoria, having heard her screams, came loping up the steps from below, wearing a nightdress and sleeping bonnet.

They called the police, who arrived in minutes, but the hoods had gone, leaving the still form of Mapleway on the ground. The police asked routine questions and, on searching Mapleway's unconscious body, found he had not been robbed. They called an ambulance, which came quickly.

As they were lifting him onto the stretcher, Mapleway opened his eyes. "You latched the door," he managed. "I saw them coming. I would have made it inside, but you latched the door . . ."

After the ambulance and police had left, she collapsed into a chair, shaking. If Mapleway hadn't been robbed, the attack had to be related in some way to the elephant. That whole business obviously wasn't over yet.

11

The phone rang several times before the sound penetrated her Seconal sleep. She raised up to answer and felt slightly ill but finally managed to get the receiver to her ear.

"Whatcha trying to pull?"

"What?"

"Cut the shit! You know goddamn well what."

"Who is this?"

"You know that, too."

She glanced at the clock. Eight straight up. The Bertini hour. People were already working. She paused and took a breath. "I don't understand," she said. "I don't understand why you're calling me. I don't understand anything."

"They plugged your goddamn elephant in and it spit it back out."

"I don't know what that means." She was waking up, finally.

"They put it together according to the print and plugged it in and the machine said nothing doing."

"But, don't you understand? I have no control over— What am I supposed to do?"

"You better find out goddamn quick."

"They gave me an envelope and I gave it to you. I didn't draw the diagram. And I didn't switch it. Or change it. Or anything. Maybe your people didn't put it together right. All I did was give you what was passed on to me."

"Was that real money you got?"

"Of course it was."

"It was real and it was what you settled for. Now, Crease wants what he paid for or somebody's gonna get hurt. Do you understand *that?*"

She hesitated and then said, "Does this explain what happened to Henry Mapleway?"

"I don't know nothing about it."

"You might have sounded a little more surprised. It only happened a few hours ago."

"I said I don't know nothing about it."

"I don't believe you."

"The Englishman was working both sides of the street. He had it coming. Now, like I said, you make a deal and you keep the deal and nothing happens. You don't pay off, things can happen . . . They know who jumped him?"

"I thought you didn't know anything about it."

"I don't. I just know he had it coming. You tell me

he got jumped, and I'm asking about it. They know who?"

"I didn't say he got jumped. You said that. And I don't know who did it. If you want to know who did it, call the police."

"Yeah, I'll do that. This is dangerous business."

"What if we just give the money back?"

"They want the elephant. The right one. You go back to the leak and get the right one, in a hurry."

"I'll talk to Beech. But what if we can't get any other drawings? What if there aren't any?"

"Who'd you say?"

Perhaps he didn't know. Had she made a mistake? "Let me see what I can find out," she said quickly.

"Do it fast. Two mistakes gets to be a problem." He hung up.

She got out of bed and called Victoria. "We've got to reach Beecher," she said. "And quick."

Victoria got the number for her. When she received no answer at his apartment, she tried his office. A male voice advised that he wasn't there and wasn't expected. She dressed and left for the hospital, leaving instructions with Victoria to try Beecher's apartment every twenty minutes.

His face was puffy and splotched with bruises; his lips were hardly recognizable. And he told her his body was all taped up because of the broken ribs. And every part of him had been in such pain that he'd felt as if he had been run over by a lorry. "I believe you'd call it a truck," he said with a little smile in his pitifully swollen eyes.

She was relieved to learn that the doctor expected

no permanent damage. Just a good solid beating administered by experienced professionals. A little something to let him know that he wasn't supposed to work both sides of the street. She brushed at his disheveled hair against the white pillow. Would Diane have smoothed his hair? She somehow had trouble picturing Diane sitting by a hospital bed, comforting a patient.

"How could they do this to you?" she asked finally, after she had told him about Bertini's call.

"It seems clear enough," he said, "now that I know about the call. The bloody elephant wouldn't fly. They knew I know Penn, and they must have decided that I was part of a scheme to take them. The sad part is, they checked out the elephant before they got around to paying me off. I don't even have money to cover my stay in this posh American hospital. Rather ironic, don't you think?"

"Please don't worry, there's plenty of money. What does worry me is that I haven't been able to get in touch with Beech."

"Keep after him."

"We can't find him anywhere. We even tried at his office."

"Surely you remembered it's best not to call him there."

"I figured since it was Saturday, it wouldn't matter."

"The security guards record incoming calls on weekends."

"Do you suppose Beecher realizes the drawing's not right?"

"I don't know."

"Will he be able to get the right one?"

"I don't know."

She began to wonder if her questions were naïve, if Mapleway did know the answers, if Diane might at least have known enough not to ask these questions. She thought she sensed a certain restraint in Mapleway's responses. Of course, he was heavily sedated, and his eyes were beginning to close as though he were dozing.

She finally decided to leave him alone. "The evening was great fun," she said. "Until . . ."

"Until I met with my reception committee?"

"I should have left the door unlatched."

"Please do so in the future. I can't understand your sudden preoccupation with latches."

"It isn't like me, is it?"

"Not at all." He was speaking with his eyes completely closed.

"I'm going to leave and let you rest. I'll send you a card that says get well soon."

"I shall look forward to reading it in good health."

She looked for a spot on his face that wasn't badly bruised. Choosing finally his temple, she kissed him lightly there. The spot was warm and damp.

He smiled without opening his eyes. "We really must reach a better understanding about things, you know." He continued smiling and then began to breathe regularly, as though he had fallen asleep.

12

When John Sturdi picked her up that night, she half expected him to comment on her hyper-anxious state. She and Victoria had spent the afternoon calling Beecher's number, to no effect. She hoped Sturdi would provide a distraction in the midst of her panic; as they got into the car, she dreaded the strain of acting normal.

They drove to a private town club, to a "small gathering," he called it, "where you'll have an opportunity to meet a few of my business associates and others involved in the California electronics game. I hope you won't find them too boring. Their wives try to discourage them from talking shop, but sometimes they get carried away."

"Don't be silly," she said. "I expect to find the California electronics jungle fascinating."

"That reminds me—did you happen to recall any more of that conversation you overheard?"

She sensed that he was watching her very closely for her reaction to his question. "No," she said. "I really don't know why I even mentioned it." His expression gave her no clue as to whether she had succeeded in quieting his curiosity.

She saw Beecher the moment they walked in. He was holding a drink in his hand and talking to a blonde with an ornate hairdo and a distinctly European manner. The blonde was also holding a drink, but she had her other hand in Beecher's hair.

When he finally noticed her standing there watching him, his face seemed to break apart for just an instant with a "what the hell are you doing here?" look. He glanced away and back and away and back, his expression making it perfectly clear that he wanted no one there to realize he knew her. She turned and went with Sturdi to circulate around the room.

She was relieved to find no one else who recognized her. As she and Sturdi approached Beecher, Sturdi said, "You two may already know each other." He said it as if he'd seen them together somewhere. Had Sturdi known Diane? The irritating doubt returned.

"Don't believe we've had the pleasure," Beecher said.

"But there has to be a first time for everything worthwhile, doesn't there?" she said.

Sturdi watched the exchange closely, as did the blonde, Inga something-or-other. She'd have to watch herself around Inga.

The group consisted of some fifteen to twenty

couples, the women, mostly wives, the men, all executive committee members. A regional branch of some technical society, sponsored and maintained by the electronic computer industry. The men were mostly middle management from industry, some from giants like IBM and NCR and some from the smaller, California-based firms, which, she gathered as she listened, were highly specialized in miniaturized computer circuitry. A few of the men held academic positions in electronics and related fields.

Sturdi seemed delighted when she expressed strong interest in it all. He discussed the men and their work freely, providing her with more of the information she needed to pull things together. Sturdi worked for Marden Microcircuits, one of the California firms. "And Beecher Grant used to—"

"Who?"

"Beecher Grant. Over there. I introduced you to him a moment ago."

"Oh, yes. Of course."

"Anyway, he used to be with us at Marden. Now he works for Harold Penn, to whom we sometimes respectfully refer as 'The Man.'"

"Why? I mean, why do you call him that?"

"If there's one real genius in California electronics circles, it's Dr. Harold Penn of Penn-Harrington Electronics."

She continued listening throughout the rather lengthy cocktail hour, occasionally exchanging quick glances with Beecher. Everyone's interest in the group seemed to be focused on an international exposition, held twice every year and coming up soon, this time in New York. Apparently this exposition was particularly important to the smaller firms. Buying decisions for months and years of future computer business were made or at least strongly influenced by exhibits at this show, and those decisions could make or break a small independent company.

She heard no mention of an elephant, but she was fascinated by the vocabulary these people used, words like anodes, diodes, semiconductors, transistors, printouts, consoles, high-density memories, bits, bites, words, words of storage, cores, digitals, analogs, microseconds, nanoseconds, channels. A whole new language. Computers had always been strange, superhuman machines with tiny lights flashing off and on and large tape reels turning, machines that did, in a few seconds, the work of thousands of men working thousands of hours, machines which when properly instructed would, among other things, print multiple images of Santa Clauses and Christmas trees, using letters and numbers in rhythmic columns and rows.

And all of this, she learned, still held true. Computers did solve gigantic problems and send people their bills and guide missiles and steer airplanes in fog—and, still, print Christmas trees. Because men somewhere had the training and skill to design them—men like the ones she was listening to. Far from being bored by their talk, she was totally caught up in it, not minding in the least that most of it was beyond her.

The cocktail hour finally began to drift toward tables for groups of twelve that had been set up on a veranda looking across the lights of the city. San Francisco was magnificent at night. Also, rather chilly. She chose a seat close to one of the sliding glass partitions in order to stay as warm as possible. Beecher and the Inga thing—Scandinavian, she'd decided—were at the same table with her and Sturdi.

As the computer talk raged on through the seafood cocktails and into the soup, she listened, fascinated.

"Looks like everybody in the Bay Area's trying to get into the memory game."

"Listen, there's a tremendous demand for a more efficient core memory unit. If somebody doesn't come up with something quick, IBM and the monolithics are going to have it all."

"Think anybody'll do it?"

"They say The Man is onto something big. And he'll unveil it at the show."

"I'll believe it when I see it," Sturdi said.

She glanced at Beecher. His expression was totally noncommittal.

"The story going around is that Penn has a new core memory component that really moves. Nanoseconds instead of microseconds."

"Horseshit! That is, if the ladies present will pardon the expression."

"That's the rumor. They're saying he can get an 80K core into less than two cubic feet—and it moves faster on less power and at much lower price per bit."

"I repeat. Horseshit! Whether the ladies pardon me or not."

"What about it, Grant? You work for him."

Beecher smiled. "No comment."

"I've heard the stories, too. It's supposed to be one hell of a unit."

"If the claims are true, he'll blow the whole memory game wide open. He could stall a semiconductor takeover for years."

"Come on, Beecher, Tell us something."

"No comment."

"Well, we've all heard the story, true or not, including his code name for the unit."

"You mean 'the elephant?'"

She felt Sturdi nudge her with an elbow.

"I hear he calls it that as a joke because it'll be so much smaller than the units in use."

"I thought he called it 'the elephant' because it was a supermemory unit."

Beecher smiled. "Maybe he calls it that for both reasons."

"There you go! Story confirmed."

Beecher grinned. "If you want to take that as confirmation, you go right ahead. I wish we had customers as easy as you."

"I'll believe it when I see it," Sturdi said again, a peculiar smile on his face.

"Listen," Beecher said. "You microcircuit jockeys oughta stay out of the memory business, anyway. Leave it to the big boys, like IBM and us."

"IBM and you? The elephant and the flea."

"We're back to the elephant."

"If Penn's got what they say he's got, he's going to be a pretty significant flea."

After the dinner dishes had been cleared, Sturdi excused himself to go to the men's room. Beecher, seeing him get up from the table, decided to join him.

She glanced across at Inga. Inga smiled, making it clear that maybe Sturdi didn't know she knew Beecher, but old Inga knew it for sure.

The conversation of the men had dominated the table. With Beecher and Sturdi away, she tuned in for a moment to the other women at the table as they discussed supermarkets, car pools, hairdressers, and elementary education, leaning forward or back, speaking in front of or behind their men.

After dessert and coffee, the talk turned again to Harry Penn. As she listened to the talk about him, she wondered if she—that is, Diane—already knew him.

"Why doesn't he ever come to these committee meetings any more?"

"He's probably sitting somewhere right now, wearing a headset, listening to everything we're saying about him."

"You think he's got this place wired?"

"I heard somewhere that he bugs half the rooms and half the phones in the Bay Area."

"What about it, Grant?"

"He gets a good laugh every time this old fairy tale gets back to him," Beecher said. "He wired one room in his own shop once, and that's how the story got started. He's the busiest guy I know just staying alive running that business.

"What about his partner? I thought Harrington was the business brain."

"Harrington died several years ago. Penn runs the whole show himself."

"What about Harrington's son?"

"Richard Harrington the Third? He's a thirty-eight-year-old surfer. He has a lovely tan."

The temperature had continued to drop on the veranda, and she was beginning to feel uncomfortable. She told Sturdi, who suggested that they try to move the group inside. But everyone seemed so relaxed and so into the spirited discussion that she accepted his jacket over her shoulders instead. She noticed Beecher and Inga watching closely as he straightened and smoothed the shoulders into place.

"I have to agree with you," a bright New York type was saying. "If there is such a thing, the Bay Area has got to be a great place for a little industrial spying."

Industrial spying! Having been preoccupied with getting warm, she had missed a little of the conversation. These two words brought her attention crashing back. The young man, aggressive and owlish, with thick horn-rims and a heavy Brooklyn accent, was expounding.

"Listen," he continued. "How many talented guys are there? Really talented. Damn few. I'll bet you can count all the ones in the Bay Area on your fingers and toes, maybe just your fingers. How many Harry Penns are there?"

"You've got a point."

"Suppose a medium-sized lab is willing to spend a little money on R and D. What's a Ph.D. straight out of Tech getting now? Fifteen? Maybe eighteen? If his feet don't touch ground, maybe twenty? Say fifteen. Now, burden is equal to salary, so it costs thirty a year to carry him. And he won't come up with anything for a year, maybe two, maybe never. He could be a lemon who interviews well.

"But let's say he's okay. Now. Suppose you're going to set up a development program to come up with something new. An elephant, for instance. Let's say four of these guys, ranging from fifteen to twenty-five, averaging twenty, and four helpers, flunkies, at half that much. You're talking four times twenty is eighty, plus four times ten makes a hundred and twenty and double that to cover burden and you're talking a quarter of a million a year. That's a megabuck in four years. And it might produce nothing."

"Your math sounds about right," Sturdi said, grinning.

"Do you know how many customers you have to find for your stuff to net a quarter of a megabuck in black ink below the bottom line? And that's just for R and D, one item on the budget."

She glanced at Beecher. An elephant for a hundred thousand was quite a bargain. She began to feel a strange sense of guilt.

"Little wonder there's industrial hanky-panky. By stealing secrets, one way or another, you get the developments for a fraction of the cost in a fraction of the time. And time is often more important than the money."

"Such as now, with the New York show coming up."
She began to feel warm.

"Well, I think you guys overdo the spy thing." An Ivy League type. "There's a lot of business intelligence practiced that's not quite espionage. You know you can get a hell of a lot of competitive information in above board ways. Conversation at a meeting like this, for instance. Or a convention. Brainpicking in legal ways. And look how much good information is published by guys dying to get into print. Or guys at universities."

"Yes, I suppose." Another straight WASP type. "Many top-flight companies have data retrieval programs for storing every little tidbit they pick up and experts who do nothing but look for it. The technical journals, conference proceedings, even *The Wall Street Journal*. And, of course, what's reported by their guys on the road."

"Well, that kind of legal intelligence may sound

good"—the kid from Brooklyn again—"but when it comes to needing stuff that'll really help you get to be one up, I still say a copied drawing, a monitored conversation, a reject piece fished out of the trash is the ticket. It may not be legal or ethical but it's being done. Wasn't some famous industrialist quoted as saying that if he could go through your trash, he could steal your business away?"

She began to feel extremely uncomfortable.

"But you never hear about criminal action being taken," said Beecher. "It's always a lawsuit. One company suing another. Never cops pulling somebody in for posing as a janitor and photographing drawings."

"Well, that's true. Most of the time."

"But not all the time. Remember the Haynes case? That was real cloak-and-dagger stuff. And they made some arrests."

She felt ill. She looked at Beecher, but he seemed calm.

"Hey, did you guys hear that one of the New York families took over Peninsula Micronics?" Brooklyn again. "*That* should bring a little excitement into Bay Area electronics."

"I heard they're planning to use it as a legitimate investment. Everybody told them computers were big. Keep your desk drawers locked, guys."

"Actually, they've got some pretty smart kids down at Peninsula. They were building a hell of an organization before they were acquired."

"I suspect these kids will be getting even smarter with their new management."

She got up out of her chair. "Excuse me." After reaching the ladies' room and closing the door, she lifted

Sturdi's jacket off her shoulders and started to hang it on a hook on the back of the door. An envelope was sticking out of an inside pocket—a brown envelope.

She locked the door and eased the envelope out of the pocket. It had already been opened at one end and pressed shut. She peeled the rubbery, pressure-sensitive seal open and shook the contents out. A large, folded sheet of paper, some sort of drawing, and, attached to it with a paper clip, a sheet from a small memo pad.

> John baby,
> Have an elephant—
> B.

She unfolded the drawing and looked at it. A complicated circuit diagram, which looked like the one she had given Bertini. In the lower right-hand corner was the nameplate: Penn-Harrington Electronics. Sturdi's repeated "I'll believe it when I see it," began to echo in her mind.

She refolded it carefully and put it back into the envelope, pressed the flap closed, and returned it to the pocket. Then she sat down on a little stool and looked in the mirror. Harry Penn, Mapleway's battered face and broken ribs, Beecher and Inga, a pile of hundred dollar bills, Bertini, a funeral, Chavez, Roger, Mr. Hodgeson, three deer, a rainslicked Sawmill Parkway, a pleasant little office in Mount Kisco . . .

Tears started down her face. Diane lived. Diane the spy.

13

Somewhere out there the phone was ringing again, trying to break through—a two-Seconal hangover this time. She could lift the receiver and bury it under a pillow, but he would only call again. Nothing that simple would make him go away.

"Hello."

"Good morning." A note of oily sweetness?

"I don't have it for you," she said. "I haven't been able to do a thing. Please. I need more time—"

"Take it easy, will ya? I didn't call about that thing."

"Then why'd you wake me up?"

"I gotta 'nuther invitation for ya."

"Invitation to what?" Why was he being so friendly?

"Same as last time. Crease wants you to come have Sunday brunch with him."

Same as last time? "When?"

"Ain't today Sunday? Today."

"What time?"

"I'll pick you up eleven-thirty."

"You don't really think I'd go anywhere in a car with you now."

"Relax. Christ, if you're worried about it, bring your neighborhood cop along. We'll be glad to give him a cuppa coffee. Jesus. I took you over there last time."

"That was last time."

"Look, I'll be in front of your place eleven-thirty, okay?"

She hesitated for a moment and heard a click. He had hung up.

She set the alarm on the clock for ten-thirty, then sank back down to finish sleeping off the effects of her second night in a row of barbiturates.

An angry whine this time. A dentist's drill or maybe a hornet, close by. She reached out and turned off the alarm. She rolled over for a moment, then gave up and got out of bed.

The phone stopped ringing as she stepped out of her shower. Victoria must have answered it in the kitchen. She went over to the phone, leaving a trail of wet footprints on the carpet. ". . . Still asleep, Mr. Grant," Victoria was saying as she picked up. "I have it, Victoria," she said. "Oh, you there, mum? Mr. Grant to speak with you." Victoria's phone clicked off.

"How do you know Sturdi?" Beecher asked.

"I met him on the plane flying out from New York last week."

"Small world. You really took me by surprise."

"I gathered as much."

"About Inga, she's—"

"I've got to talk to you. Did you hear about Mapleway?"

"Yes, and I don't know what to make of it."

"Bertini called yesterday. The elephant drawing I gave him wasn't right. He said they checked it out and it wouldn't work."

"That's impossible! How could they possibly have checked it out so fast?"

"You're asking me?"

"Even if they had every man, woman, and child in the neighborhood down there stringing cores, I still don't see how they could have checked it so soon. They must be better than I expected. I figured we'd have more time."

"What does that mean? Did you know it wasn't going to work?"

"I just estimated it'd take them a week or two at best, and then"—he hesitated—"then, I figured them for a nice gesture of thanks for a job well done."

"What about Henry Mapleway?"

"They know he's your pal. They're using him to get you to run scared."

"I asked Bertini about Henry. He said Henry, as he put it, plays both sides of the street."

"Mapleway knows most everybody around, including Penn. Knowing everybody is what he does for a living."

"Well, with the Mapleway attack Friday night and

Bertini's call Saturday morning, I am a little unnerved. And that's not all. Bertini called this morning. I've been invited to brunch again."

"Eat hearty. I understand the Godfather sets out quite a spread."

"Who told you that?"

"You did."

"I'm terrified about going this time."

"You'll be safe. Bertini's an excellent driver."

"You're not very funny at all. I'm sure you know that."

"I can't believe they'd lay a glove on you. Bertini's too hot for you. Then, on the other hand, they want the elephant. Bad."

"And that's all? Just like that?"

"Inga's the daughter of one of Penn's international contacts."

"I understand perfectly. Business is business."

"You enjoy yourself with John Sturdi?"

"He was charming. And an absolute gentleman."

"Glad to hear it. See you later, after you get back from brunch."

"Wait. What do I say to them at brunch?"

"Wear long lashes and bat them up and down a lot. You don't know anything. But you'll try and find out more."

"What *is* the story? And what are we going to do?"

"Try and get the right drawing. Before they do something else ugly."

As she hung up, parts of the conversation—small details, inferences, intonations—nagged at her. The question about expecting to have more time. He had raised it, and then been funny about it. And she'd wanted to mention the envelope in Sturdi's pocket, and then been afraid to do it. Elephants for everybody! Hooray! And Inga. She'd have to keep in mind that Diane probably wouldn't give Inga a second thought.

She looked at the clock. Eleven A.M. That made it two in the afternoon in Mount Kisco. Sunday afternoon in Mount Kisco. There, she'd be listening to good music and working the *Times* Double Crostic. And her good friend and suitor, Roger, the real-estate agent, would be out selling houses. Sunday afternoon was his best day. And later he'd very likely come over, flushed with the success of a big sale, and take her out for supper and maybe a movie.

Instead, she was getting dressed to get into a big black automobile, with a greasy hood who would drive her to brunch with a mysterious figure outside the law who already knew her. And Roger? Roger was probably out showing a customer the old Lanigan place.

Bertini was the picture of nervous excitement. As he drove with her sitting demurely next to him, he was like a teenager on his first date. She had caused him a major agony by not walking out of the house until almost a quarter to twelve, despite his impatient beeps on the horn. And then she'd started to get into the back seat, and he'd made a fuss about having her in front. He was obviously on his best Sunday behavior.

She was hungry. After dressing, she had come downstairs to the tempting aroma of bacon. She and Victoria chatted briefly, despite the insistent horn toots from outside, and she resisted even sampling the breakfast Victoria was laying out. She wanted to maintain a respectable appetite for "brunch with the Godfather."

They drove for over thirty minutes, the ride high-lighted by the conversational inanities that were Bertini's idea of trying to be friendly. They arrived at an enormous house, located very high on a hill and commanding a view of the Golden Gate Bridge. The house was surrounded by a massive wall of matching stone, its upper edge trimmed in ornate steel spikes. An attendant pulled open a steel gate as they approached; the metal lattice over the gate contained the sculpted letters: "Bay Vista."

Bertini stopped the car under the archway leading to the front entrance, and she allowed him to come around and help her out of the car. They walked onto the portico. As they approached the heavy double doors, she noted a shiny brass nameplate on the right-hand door engraved with "Anthony J. Croece." Crease. Bertini tapped with the knocker, and the door opened.

"Hello, my dear. So nice to see you again. Please come in." He was a tiny man, less than five feet tall, thin, and small-boned. He wore rimless glasses; his fair skin seemed tightly stretched across his cheekbones. His hair was thin and a gray-beige in color, combed straight back from his face so that it accentuated his pointed nose. The vastness of the house around him seemed set off by his smallness. "I hope you're very hungry," he said. "As you know, Sunday brunch is something of a tradition with us. And, just as we do many other things, we take it quite seriously."

"I'm famished," she said. She had to look down at him.

"Very good." He led her and Bertini across the echoing foyer and into a dining room. The long table had three place settings clustered around one end, and a sideboard held an array of food that would have been impressive in a large hotel.

After they were seated, he offered her the choice of a Persian melon section or sliced California oranges. She chose the oranges, which were served from a silver tureen by a wordless young Chinese woman in a native costume. The main course was kippers and scrambled eggs, delicately prepared and garnished with a tiny rice pilaf. Hot breads, rolls, muffins, and croissants were brought around, along with an assortment of jams and jellies that glittered in their silver dishes. Coffee was drawn from a large antique silver urn. A huge wheel of cheese, fragile Italian shell pastries covered with powdered sugar, and fresh fruit were served with it. She had never seen such large, perfect pears. Croece took one of the pears and dug a few bites from it with a teaspoon.

She kept expecting Croece to mention the elephant, but conversation throughout breakfast was pleasantly social. Bertini stuffed himself. The Chinese servant seemed to know it wasn't necessary to give him dainty portions.

She had become fascinated by an element of flavoring in the flaky little pastries, nutmeg or anise or something, and kept breaking off a little more and a little more. She was dabbing the powdered sugar from her mouth with a napkin when she noticed that Croece was staring quietly at her with a peculiarly intense expression. She suddenly felt very frightened and very alone. His eyes were gray, almost colorless, a little like the color of his hair.

His expression softened and he said, "Excuse me,

my dear, for staring at you, but you're very lovely. Even more so than I remembered you. Isn't she lovely, Pasquale?"

Bertini had to get a large bite of cheese under better control before answering. "Yeah, she is."

She felt herself blush. "Well, thank you, both of you."

"We need your help in finishing what is started," Croece said suddenly. "We trust you appreciate the urgency of the matter."

Although he had spoken in his characteristic soft manner, his emphasis on the word "urgency" made her tremble. "I can't understand it," she said. "The drawing I got for you should have been—"

"The details are not important, my child," he said. "We have every confidence in your ability to fulfill your commitment in this matter. Again I must emphasize the urgency of it. We don't make a practice of making bad investments. We have been exercising restraint, but the time for restraint is rapidly running out. The exposition in New York is just over four weeks away. Sometimes, in the interest of business, we are forced to take steps we would prefer to avoid. I hope we understand each other."

"I'll certainly see what I can find out as quickly as possible." She had difficulty getting the words out.

He seemed to relax in his chair. The business meeting was over. Obviously satisfied with the message he had delivered and its impression on her, he returned to small talk. After a little more coffee, they took a walk around the grounds, enjoying the sun, the view, the landscaping. Formal gardens were arranged within an embattlement, the wall open only on the bluff side toward the vista of the bay.

"Pasquale may take you home now," Croece said finally, "and we'll look forward to seeing you again, perhaps when we can enjoy celebrating success in our area of mutual interest. Let us hope that will be very soon."

"You get the message?" Bertini said as they drove away.

"I guess so."

"Croece has got a bundle tied up in this computer thing. And he don't like losers."

"All I can do is pass a drawing along."

"You can do more than that. You can persuade somebody. Know what I mean?"

They drove in silence for a while. He flipped on the radio, and hard rock blared into the car. He quickly cut back on the volume and fished around on the dial until he found some soft music. "You know," he said, "I could really do you a lot of good."

She didn't respond.

"I really could," he said. "And I'll tell you something else. I go for you. You're a good-looking head."

She remained quiet.

"And I'll tell you something else. I'm not that bad. I'm really not. And I could take you anywhere you want to go. Anywhere. Just say the word."

She waited, wondering what he would say next.

"How about inviting me in when we get back to your place?"

"I'm afraid I—"

"Wait. If that sounded a little pushy, maybe we could go out. You know. Spend the day together. Or the evening. Go anywhere you'd like to go. Name it."

He was beginning to reach her a little. Then she

remembered who he was. And she thought about Henry Mapleway. "I'm afraid I have plans for the rest of today."

"What about tomorrow?"

"Then, too."

"What do I have to do to . . . make friends with you?"

"A good beginning would be to never call me on the phone before twelve noon," she said, looking at the phone contraption beneath the dashboard.

She'd said it too glibly. He looked hurt for a moment, then his face tightened up. He'd wasted his time, made a fool of himself. And he wasn't happy about it.

They drove without conversation for a while. As they pulled up in front of the house he said, "I'll be in touch in a couple of days. You better come up with something. Like he said, it's urgent."

She wanted to say something at least slightly friendly, but she could see the scowl back on his face. As she got out, she said, "Thank you for the ride."

"Don't mention it," he snapped and pulled away.

In the house she found Beecher in the library, a drink in his hand, watching a ball game on TV. "How was it?" he asked.

"He invited me over to frighten me, and he succeeded. Beecher, I'm really scared. He wants the thing and he wants it quick."

"I'll see if I can't get the right drawing tomorrow. Penn'll be away in the morning. It'll be easy."

"What was wrong with the other one?"

"I'll try and find out tomorrow," he said. "This is today. Let's relax and enjoy it."

"Where's Victoria?"

"I gave her the afternoon off."

"Think you can tear yourself away from the game?"

He put down his drink and came over to her and slipped his arms around her. "Don't pick a fight you can't win."

"I'm surprised you're not out with that little Danish pastry."

"That sounds like something I'd expect your sister to say."

"It does at that, doesn't it?" It was true. Diane wouldn't have said it. "Why don't you fix me a drink while I get undressed and get a few thousand dollars to spread on the floor?"

"Are you telling me that we established a new precedent with that money?"

"Why not?" she said. "Think big." The game had to go on.

14

Fisherman's Wharf. A great new place to be alone and think. Boats of various sizes bobbing in the water, and groups of people, chattering and preoccupied. A bite of lunch at DiMaggio's. "DiMaggio's is a tourist trap." But it had been good. And she was still almost a tourist, anyway. She had plenty of time to become a hardened native.

She was tired from the walk down the hill to the wharf area. It had seemed close on the map, but she had once again underestimated the San Francisco hills. But she'd felt like walking among strangers, enjoying the sunshine and the breeze off the water.

And from the Wharf to the Embarcadero, not really

scenic but still fascinating. She had always loved big ships. Yet, in all the years spent near Manhattan, she had been down to the docks along the Hudson only once. She thought back to that rainy morning when she and Diane had driven down the West Side Highway to deliver Aunt Flossie to her tourist-class stateroom for a cruise to the Caribbean. Someone once told her a person could fly to London in the time it took to get the *Queen Elizabeth* away from the dock and past the Statue of Liberty. Perhaps. And perhaps it was just that majestic slowness that gave a big ship its charm.

She continued along the Embarcadero, the wide street, the ships, the massive cargo terminals between the ships, the glimpses of water between these buildings. She stopped to watch the unloading activity on one of the freighters, the towering crane and the hulking pallets of cargo. Was there anyone, anywhere, who wouldn't get hooked on watching it?

So much to think about. Brunch the day before, and the message delivered over kippers and eggs. Urgency. Croece hoped she appreciated the urgency . . . Beecher said he'd get the drawings. Harry Penn would be away during the morning . . . At least Henry Mapleway was much improved. Visiting him that morning, she had found him sitting up in his hospital bed, quite chipper, "staring like a blithering idiot at your crassly commercial American telly." He would be leaving the "unconscionably priced" hospital shortly. "And tell me, my dear. Where are you going from here?"

"I thought I'd go down to Fisherman's Wharf and have a bite of lunch and walk around."

"Surely you jest. Fish and chips doesn't sound like you at all."

But she had loved the food. And the air and the sun and the faces and the atmosphere and the ships in regal quietude all along the Embarcadero. If it wasn't a Diane thing, she just wouldn't tell anyone the next time she chose to come back.

When she got back to the house, she found Beecher having a drink and chatting with Victoria. She greeted them and then rushed upstairs to dress for the evening's festivities. Before they left the house, Beecher pulled another brown envelope from his inside jacket pocket and handed it to her. "When the heavy calls again, give him this one. This should make them all smiles."

They had dinner at an impeccable French restaurant where several people knew and greeted them. As adept as she was becoming at returning the helloes of people who knew Diane, she still often wondered what she would do if one of them said, "I'm one of your very closest friends. Who am I?"

After drinks and dinner with wine, they drove to the San Francisco Museum of Art and joined a glittering crowd, the benefit set, there for an opening of an exhibit, "new" works of Impressionists and post-Impressionists, on visit from the U.S.S.R. People were arriving in droves, beautiful people and just plain rich people; kinky types in ruffled shirts, and women in everything from formal gowns with full-length gloves to skimpy little jean suits. Art lovers. Another segment of Diane's crowd.

Yet as the mob continued to pour into the museum, the magnificent art went all but unnoticed. Temporary bars had been set up in the huge central gallery, and frantic bartenders were sloshing liquor into plastic glasses. Unless the people who snatched at the drinks so eagerly had been inside the Hermitage or the Pushkin

Museum in Russia, they had presumably never seen these paintings.

Many people knew her, and she reacted to their friendly advances instinctively, hugging or kissing or simply shaking hands as the approaching friends telegraphed their intentions, responding to the "hello, Dianes" by approximating Diane's conversational style as best she could. She felt loose and relaxed. Beecher had given her the new drawing. And the evening's drinking was getting to her.

She managed a glimpse here and there of some of the art in the exhibit, restraining the impulse to linger in the Cézanne corner, to which one painting, *The Smoker,* had drawn her like a magnet. She had always avoided crowd scenes at museums or galleries, going instead to enjoy the works being shown in thoughtful solitude. She'd come back to this exhibit another day.

"Hey, Lanigan!" The young man who had led her into the water-pipe circle Friday night.

He embraced her, then introduced himself to Beecher. She managed to catch his first name, at least. Joey.

"How about we reassemble at your place tonight when we leave here?" he said to her. "That last time was the absolute limit."

She looked at Beecher and then back at Joey. "I wouldn't have it any other way."

"See you at around twelve, doll, and I'll bring the troops."

After he walked away, she turned to Beecher and said, "Party, party!"

"You're too much, Diane," he said. "Do you know everybody in town?"

Beecher left her for a few minutes to get fresh drinks. A conservatively dressed man with a well-shaped bald head and scholarly-looking eyeglasses greeted her with warmth and familiarity. Someone else she should know well. The trim, beautifully dressed woman with him, apparently his wife, also greeted her by first name. The man seemed unusually intrigued—was he one of Diane's older admirers? Yet he wasn't really old, just bald; his skin was smooth, and the body that wore the formal clothes so gracefully was lean and muscular. And he was looking at her the way she had looked at the Cézanne.

Beecher returned, pleased but not rurprised to see the couple. He called him Harry, and her, Dorothy.

Harry Penn? She listened closely to the conversation, deciding finally that this had to be him, Beecher's boss, the one real genius in California electronics circles, "The Man"—the man, she thought, whose best work they were stealing and peddling all over California.

She felt even more uncomfortable than she had on Saturday night. Watching Beecher, she wondered what sort of conflict might be working on his mind. His rapport with Penn seemed perfect. "Anything yet on the Star of India?" he asked Penn at one point. The Star of India. Surely another code name for something. More confidential material within Beecher's reach.

She studied Penn, finding him warm and straightforward, completely trusting of Beecher. A perfect quarry. As the conversation drifted further into business matters, she thought she could recognize signs of Penn's brilliance. But why these frequent glances, which were making her so uneasy?

They spent much of the evening with the Penns.

And after calling Victoria to tell her to expect an unknown quantity of people for twelve midnight, she invited the Penns. Mrs. Penn declined, her smile suggesting that Diane should know from long experience that it wasn't necessary to extend them an invitation to one of her midnight blasts.

They left the museum in time to get back to her house by eleven-thirty, before any guests were to arrive. They were too late. A roaring party was under way. Victoria was in her element, maintaining a steady supply of food and drink to the mélange of twenty or thirty young people. Her friend Joey wanted to know if she had any grass.

She referred the request to Victoria with a wave of her hand and a fleeting memory of a meeting about drug abuse she had attended in Bedford Hills a few weeks back. In a matter of minutes Victoria had descended the stairs with the black velvet purse, and the brass pipe was circulating among six or seven people on the floor.

Beecher, seeing that the party was just getting wound up, said something about having a tough Tuesday ahead and left her to her "art lovers." She wished they would all leave, but knew it was too much to hope for. Sensing, however, that she could disappear and not be missed, she wandered out of the living room and up the stairs to her bedroom. As she entered, she was greeted warmly by a bearded young man just peeling off a turtleneck sweater and a young girl with long straight blonde hair who was almost undressed. She suggested that they try the room across the hall. They accepted her offer and left, carrying their shoes and clothes with them.

She sat on the edge of her bed for a moment and

then checked the drawer for the envelope Beecher had given her. Downstairs, the stereo had been started with a record whose heavily rhythmic beat seemed to shake the house. She undressed and slipped into the big wonderful bed, trying not to think of Harry Penn. She pulled the covers over her head and finally tunneled her head under the pillow. But the music penetrated even the pillow. Why didn't they cut the goddamn thing off and get the hell out?

Goddamn? Get the hell out? She was beginning to think in Diane, the way she had once begun to think in French.

She lay quietly in the darkness, listening to the music, finding that she was beginning to adjust to the volume. A memory from childhood skittered across her mind, a suddenly clear memory of a night when she and Diane lay awake in their bedroom as one of Quick Sam Lanigan's liveliest shindigs roared away downstairs.

She turned from one side to the other, resting but not sleeping, upstairs from a party. Finally she got up, turned on the light, slipped on slacks and a shirt, and went back down to the living room. The crowd had thinned to ten or twelve people who sat around, either stoned or drunk, listening to or ignoring the music, which was still throbbing away. Leftover food, dishes, and glasses were all over the room.

She glanced at a clock and noticed that it was almost three o'clock. She looked for Victoria and, not finding her, went downstairs to the door of her room and knocked.

After a moment, "Come in, mum."

Victoria sat up and switched on a small lamp as she entered the room and perched on the edge of the bed.

"I met Harry Penn tonight."

"Oh, mum, I'm afraid I failed to tell you—"

"He seems one of the most decent men I've met since getting out here. Victoria, I'm not sure I can go on stealing his drawings and selling them for money to the hood element. I can't imagine what Diane was doing."

"Please, mum, there's something else you need to know."

"I'm afraid to ask."

"Diane knew Dr. Penn very well indeed. She was seeing him before Mapleway introduced her to Beecher Grant."

"She never mentioned Penn when I saw her."

"Oh, I'm sure she would have gotten to it, luv. Given enough time. She found it all terribly exciting at first. Stealing secrets from her own lover. Then she became attracted to Grant. She began to have terrible bouts with her conscience about the unsavory dealings she had involved *him* in. And she was fearful she'd get caught—if not by the authorities, at least by Dr. Penn. And there was the question of not seeing Penn any more. How could she want Grant and continue with Penn? She became horribly, horribly confused. That's when she decided she needed you."

"But Penn's married." What hadn't Diane done? "Victoria. How and where did Penn and Diane see each other alone?"

"Dr. Penn traveled quite a bit. Diane would fly and meet him in other cities."

"And I've got to deal with all of these relationships she established—and all of the problems . . . Victoria? What am I going to do?"

126

"First, I think you'd better give the drawing Mr. Grant brought you to Mr. Bertini and hope for the best. That should be the end of that. If you don't, I'm afraid Mr. Bertini may do something bloody serious."

"And what about Penn?"

"Perhaps he'll not find out about the drawing. And with luck, you should be able to work the other matters out."

She sat silent for a moment. Then, "Victoria?"

"Yes, mum."

"What does Diane do when she begins to feel that she just can't cope any more? I mean, when she feels like the whole world is about to come crashing down on her."

"Why, she goes on secret holiday, luv."

"You mean, she goes away? Where to?"

"Well, if it's just for a few days, she goes to a little place down the coast around Carmel."

"Does she go alone?"

"Well, sometimes, but it would be nice if she took me with her."

"Tomorrow, let's clean this place up and pack and go."

"Oh, yes, mum."

She stood up, feeling better. "Sorry if I disturbed you."

"Oh, you didn't disturb me, luv, not at all. I was rather expecting you."

15

Bertini time. She was already awake in anticipation of his call. She glanced at the clock as she turned over to reach for the phone. He was prompt, as usual.

"I have what you're looking for," she said.

"You'd better believe it." His voice was heavy with meaning. He still hadn't given up.

"I have a new drawing for you," she said quickly. "Are you parked in front of the house?"

"Long as you got the drawing, why're ya—"

"I'll bring you the envelope."

"Hey, whatcha being like this—"

She hung up. Then she slipped on the slacks and shirt she'd worn the night before, leaving the shirttail out and her hair disheveled.

She opened the door a few inches and held the envelope out through the crack. He slid his foot in through the opening as he took the envelope.

"Please move your foot."

"Invite me in."

"Why can't you be nice like you were Sunday?"

"Because that got me exactly nowhere."

"Well, neither will this. Will you please move your foot?"

"You don't know what you're missing."

"I have a vivid imagination. Now, come on, be nice and move your foot."

"Nice guys finish last."

"Either you cool it or I call Croece."

"He ain't listed."

"I have the number."

"Where the hell did you get it?"

"Do you think we tell you everything?"

He hesitated, apparently confused. "This drawing's gotta be right, or there's gonna be trouble."

"I don't expect to have to hear from you again. Please move your foot."

He slid his foot back, and she pushed the door shut and twisted the deadlatch. She returned to her room, undressed, and slid back into her bed to wonder about Croece's phone number and think about how she would act the next time she was around Harry Penn.

She got up later and found Victoria putting the house back together. They called Diane's travel agent and reserved a little house on the shoreline near Carmel. Around midafternoon, without calling anyone, they packed a few things and left.

The drive down was exhilarating. The scenery was

all new to her, and she found herself as excited by it as she had been by her first glimpse of San Francisco. Diane's California. They arrived in Carmel, picked up a key, shopped for a few days' provisions, and settled into the brightly painted little house looking out over the Pacific. She loved its tiny yard, exotic greenery and flowers, even the slightly musty smell inside the place. A vacation smell. She had returned from a week of vacation in the Poconos less than two weeks before—it *had* been less than two weeks, hadn't it?—and still she felt an urgent need to get away. As Victoria put it, "There's nothing quite like being on holiday when being on holiday is what you need. Right, luv?"

This was Diane's place to hide. It wasn't Diane's place to play. It seemed to Victoria that the whole world was Diane's place to play. Victoria felt she'd done less to earn her housekeeper's pay while she worked for Diane than almost anyone she knew, because Diane was so seldom home. Always somewhere else, some island or resort or European city. Then there had been the skiing trips to Colorado or Switzerland. She'd even been East several times—without, apparently, ever having quite gotten around to calling Mount Kisco.

But when Diane wanted to just catch up, to vegetate, she did it in one of these little houses by the Pacific. And she could see why Diane liked it as she chatted and had a bite of supper with Victoria and then stood outside in the coolish night air, watching the crashing surf, dimly lit by an early moon. Relieved that the pressure from Bertini was finally over, she would remember that moment of ocean and sky for a long time.

When she went back inside, Victoria made tea—a new kind of nightcap for California. She watched television for a few minutes and went to bed early. Something else new for California. And she slept well. No pills, no dreams, no restlessness. Another first.

The next day was perfect after touches of early fog burned off, and she reveled in the wondrous perfection of the sun and breeze and surroundings. She spent the afternoon watching from a distance as sleek, tanned surfers did their thing, hanging back, waiting for suitable swells of water and riding them in, perched atop their boards almost by some miracle of antigravity, falling at last, and dogpaddling back out to the fringe where the waves formed.

She took Victoria and drove into Carmel to a movie that night, noticing during the drive back that the perfect sky had clouded over. And the next day she was awakened by rain, sheets of rain that buffeted the little house. She relaxed in bed for a long time after waking up and listened to it, the first rain she'd heard since coming to California. She got up finally, and spent the rest of the day talking with Victoria.

During these conversahons, she relived the meeting with Penn in the light of what she had learned about Diane's relationship with him. How many other married men had Diane known intimately? Was he special? Little wonder he had looked at her with such concentrated intensity at the museum. What would she say if he called to arrange a meeting? What would she do if they were alone?

And as she thought about Penn, she also thought about Beecher. She had been worried that he and Diane might have developed some private sexual practice, an idiosyncrasy or even a fetish, that she couldn't possibly know about. She was so inexperienced in such matters. But no—surely she'd have noticed if he was suspicious.

Playing the Diane game with him was the one aspect of the whole charade she liked unequivocally. She could easily understand Diane's attraction.

And she thought about the elephant. She'd had no choice, really, about handing it over. Beecher had given it to her to pass on. Victoria had encouraged her. And Croece and Bertini had made their positions clear. She nevertheless felt extreme pangs of guilt. She doubted that she could live with it indefinitely and still keep herself together.

Sunshine came flooding back the next day, and she returned to the beach to walk along the edge of the water for what seemed miles. She was feeling much better. Things had begun to fall into place and she felt she'd made up her mind about what to do. She was almost ready to go back.

But the day after that was perfect again; the surf was up, and she again spent hours, wondering how the surfers knew to come, how they knew when the water was right. And on the next day, which was Sunday, Victoria advised against driving back because of the Sunday freeway traffic. Monday was picture-perfect, so they took still another day. When Tuesday dawned cool and gray, they cleaned up and packed and headed back.

She was thoughtful and quiet during the ride north. Her conversation with Victoria had been just a little strained since that morning, when she'd told Victoria what she intended to do. Victoria clearly disapproved. But she was resolute. It was, she had decided, the only alternative she could live with.

They pulled the car into the garage and walked toward the door leading into the house. Before she could get the key into the lock, the door swung open and there stood Bertini, his face twisted into a dark scowl. As she backed away from him, he reached out and grabbed her wrist, yanking her roughly through the door. "Where the hell you been?" he shouted. "We been waiting around here a day and a half. Almost two days." Two men materialized from behind him, rushed through the door, grabbed Victoria and pulled her into the house.

"What are you doing here?" she said as they forced Victoria into a chair. "What do you want from me? I gave you the drawing." Her eyes began to fill with tears.

"That drawing was another turkey. You got any idea what the hell kinda game you and your friends are playing?"

"I gave you what they gave me."

Bertini slapped her. "Maybe I can do ya a favor and knock a little sense into ya. You already passed the point of just getting on people's nerves. That show's just a couple weeks off and we got to have that drawing. Unnerstand?"

Her face burned where his hand had landed. "That wasn't necessary," she said.

"We gotta have the drawing."

The tall hood said quietly, "Slick, you make a mistake letting her string you along the way you been doing."

"I'll handle it," Bertini said. He stepped closer to her. "Maybe you'd rather they let somebody besides me be your contact," he said. "Somebody who don't think you're such a good-looking head. Somebody who could care less. Like maybe my two friends here. You know what I mean?"

She thought she detected a trace of uncertainty and genuine concern in his comment. Was he jeopardizing himself by his leniency with her? "Let me call Mapleway," she said. "Maybe he knows what's going on."

"Forget Mapleway. We already talked to him, and he don't know nothing." Then, in a lower voice. "He's upstairs."

"Upstairs?"

"You can go to him in a minute. We're leaving. I'll be here in the morning for the drawing. The right one. Tomorrow's it, Y'unnerstand?" He motioned to the other two men and then followed them out the front door.

Mapleway was naked, tied on her bed spreadeagled, his arms and legs lashed to the four bedposts with pantyhose. His mouth was tightly gagged with two more pairs of her pantyhose, one for stuffing and one for binding, and his belly was spotted with black cigarette smudge marks.

While Victoria untied him, she went downstairs and called Beecher at his office.

"Where on earth have you been?" he asked.

"I went away for a few days to hide and try to catch up. Listen, we've got to—"

"You might have let me know. I thought you weren't going to do that any more."

You mean it's not the first time? "Please listen. The drawing you gave me was another dud, and we've got to do something. Beecher, I'm terribly frightened . . ." She broke into sobs.

"Sounds like it would be lots of fun," he said.

"What?"

"Maybe we could play a little golf."

"Beecher, what are you talking about? . . . Oh, God, you can't talk."

"You're right about that."

"Beecher, you've got to call me back right away when it's safe. Please hurry."

"Sounds great. Get back to you later." He hung up.

When he didn't call within five minutes, she poured a glass of straight vodka over ice and began drinking. Victoria appeared, followed by Mapleway, who also poured a drink. The vodka helped, but Mapleway's stories didn't—stories he had heard about the behavior and practices of the California families, stories which made his own sufferings seem minor.

When Beecher finally called an hour later, she described her homecoming and asked how he could have given her not one but two bad drawings.

"Penn is no fool," he explained. "He keeps obsolete drawings with up-to-date designations in the proper places to be intentionally misleading. He likes to anticipate things and keep his edge. Since I'm a sales type and not a technical expert, he even had me fooled. With the show almost here, Harry decided to clue me in on this last week—so I knew Bertini would start getting nasty. But, of course, I couldn't reach you."

"What should we do?"

"I'll go back to the office tonight. This time I'll get the real thing. I'll come right over after I leave."

"Beecher, I'm not sure I can go on with this whole business."

"Pull yourself together. I promise you the next one will get them off our necks. Trust me."

"I'm not sure you should trust *me*."

"What's that supposed to mean?"

"I don't know. I think I've lost my stomach for this whole stinking mess."

"We're finished with it. Tomorrow, we can relax."

She remained silent.

"They seem to like using Mapleway as their whipping boy. I think we need to get him off someplace where he's safe."

"But why? I thought you said we were finished."

"We are. This drawing will be the right one. But that bunch can be impossible to predict. Why take chances? He's absorbed enough. I figure you and I can share the cost. It'll be a paid vacation. He'll love it."

She paused. "Where did you have in mind?"

"London, leaving tomorrow."

"I'll tell him. Anything else?"

"Harry gave me two tickets to the film festival at the Palace tomorrow night."

Was he serious?

"A good way to celebrate," Beecher continued. "And I hear the advance reviews are even favorable."

She needed more vodka.

"See you tonight," he said. "Have your travel agent handle Pinky's reservations."

"Beecher?"

"See you tonight."

She hung up the phone and turned to Mapleway and Victoria. "Guess what, Henry," she said. "You've just been awarded a free trip home." As she watched the confusion spread across his face, she refilled her glass.

16

Having awakened by instinct, and in spite of the sedation, she lay on her side, watching the minute hand of the clock move toward eight. Next to the phone was another brown envelope, sealed at one end, just like its predecessors. But this one was the elephant, the real elephant. She would take Beecher's word for it. She wondered if he'd also given a copy to John Sturdi.

Beecher had come at around ten the night before and spent nearly two hours quieting the three of them down, assuring them the new drawing was, at last, the elephant, and explaining the desirability of Mapleway's getting out of sight even though there should be no further problems. He finally left, taking Mapleway with him. He would pick Mapleway up at his place in the morning and drive him to the airport.

As the hour of eight approached, she began anticipating the ring as she had so many times before. At eight sharp she heard a smashing of glass on a lower floor. Wondering what else could possibly happen, she got up, slipped on a robe, and went downstairs. A hand came through the opening in the door where the glass had been and released the deadlatch. The door opened and Bertini came in, followed by the same two men.

"Get me the drawing," Bertini said.

She went upstairs without speaking and returned with the envelope. "You didn't have to smash the window," she said. "I would have opened the door."

"You can get it fixed." He took the envelope. "Louie and Sally gonna stay here while I get a quick check on this drawing. Good drawing, no problems. Okay? You might fix 'em some coffee. They been sitting up all night out here on the street."

"Strong and black," said the tall one.

"I'll call soon as I get an answer," Bertini said. "You better hope it's a good one." He opened the door and left.

Victoria made a pot of coffee and set the table for the two men, who sat down and began drinking and talking in Italian while she and Victoria huddled together in the library, their arms folded, in direct view of the men, as the taller one had insisted. After an hour or so, Victoria ventured into the kitchen, got two cups of coffee, and brought them back to the library.

The morning dragged on. She and Victoria sat in almost complete silence, wondering about the continuous, usually low but sporadically boisterous foreign dialogue coming from the kitchen.

The phone rang once, a few minutes after eleven. The taller man answered it, said, "She ain't here just now," and hung up. It rang again at almost one and he answered again. "Yeah?" . . . "Okay." He hung up, nodded to his partner, and the two of them left without comment.

She and Victoria jumped up and watched through the broken pane as the two men got into their car and headed down the hill. As soon as it was out of sight, she went into the library, looked up a phone number, and dialed it.

17

She had no idea how to handle the call. She knew only
that she'd made up her mind to go ahead with it. She
glanced up at Victoria, whose expression suggested that
the phone call could be a terrible mistake.

"Penn-Harrington. Good morning."

"Mr. Penn, please."

"I'll give you his secretary."

"Mr. Penn's office." Another pleasant voice.

"May I speak with him, please?"

"I'm sorry, Mr. Penn is away. May I ask who's
calling?"

"When will he return?"

"Not for a week. He left for Europe this morning,

and he plans to stop in New York on the way back. May I ask who's calling?"

"This is Diane Lanigan. Could I make an appointment to see him as soon as he returns?"

"Oh, hello, Miss Lanigan. This is Sue. You know, I didn't recognize your voice."

"I guess I'm a little out of it today."

"May I ask what you wish to see him about? He always asks me."

"Just tell him it's extremely important. If you tell him that, I'm sure he'll see me."

The secretary hesitated. "We're expecting him back next Thursday. Could you come Friday at ten?"

"Could I come Thursday?"

"That'll be his first day back, and he's going to be swamped. The show's only two weeks off, which is why he's stopping in New York. Friday would really be much better."

"Friday morning?"

"Friday at ten. We'll see you then, Miss Lanigan. I have it penciled in and I'll give him your message."

The name on the bow of the ship was wonderfully exotic: *Star of India*. Something familiar about that name. Beyond it, in the middle of the Bay, if she remembered correctly, was Alcatraz Island. She continued her walk along the Embarcadero, studying the occasional ships, old freighters mostly, and the archway entrances into the warehouse between them.

She would take full blame, full responsibility, explaining to them that she had persuaded Beecher to get the drawings completely against his will, pleading, if necessary, for some sort of amnesty for him. After all, he couldn't really be held accountable . . . She turned around and started walking slowly back toward Fisherman's Wharf.

Perhaps she should tell Beecher what she was going to do, even tell him she knew about the drawing he'd given Sturdi. Then give him the chance to get the hell out of there. After all, he did have fifty thousand dollars that *she* knew of, and no real responsibilities. He could break for Europe and become a ski bum . . . .

As she approached the *Star of India* again, the coincidence suddenly registered. Beecher's question to Penn at the museum. What sort of exotic cargo would one find coming off ships that had returned, presumably, from the Far East? She smiled at the guard near the warehouse entrance. He was a plain little man in a dark-green shirt and pants with a badge on his shirt pocket. He sat in a straight chair, leaning back against the wall, his arms folded, watching traffic, particularly her. She walked on by him and then turned back. "Is it your job just to sit here all day and guard the entrance to the warehouse?"

"I guess you could call it that." He smiled, obviously enjoying her attention. "Most of 'em up and down here got 'em. Somebody could walk in off the street and carry something off. If they could find anything they could lift."

"What's it like in there? Just sort of a typical warehouse?"

"Take a look."

She walked over to the entrance to the warehouse, which was several feet beyond the archway, and looked down the vastness of the enclosed area, orderly aisles lined with crates and cartons, some extremely large, all neatly stacked on wooden platforms. She came back over to him. "I know this is kind of an odd request, but I'd love to go in and walk around. I won't bother anything."

"What for?"

"No particular reason. I'm a tourist and I've never been to San Francisco before or to any place where they load and unload oceangoing ships, especially from the Far East, and I just sort of wanted to get an idea of what it looked like."

"The only problem is insurance. If they drop something on you or run over you, you ain't covered and I'm to blame."

"I'll be careful. Looks quiet in there right now."

"Yeah, they're probably taking a break. They take lots of breaks."

"Would you mind terribly?" She widened her smile.

"Don't stay long. Come back and talk to me some more."

She entered the warehouse area and began wandering down one of the long aisles. At a cross aisle about halfway down the length of the room and to her right, seated on the floor in an open area near the ship, were three young men in work clothes, talking and smoking, and holding soft drinks. They studied her, pleasantly surprised but startled to see her there. She wanted to walk over to the dock and look at the ship from up close, but their ogling stares made her self-conscious. After a clumsy moment of hesitation, she moved on toward the far end of the room, walking more quickly. She came to another cross aisle and turned left. Then she turned left again and started back toward the entrance.

A large crate caught her attention and she stopped.

It was a crate made up of rough-hewn teakwood slats, two or three inches wide and spaced about four inches apart. The contents appeared to be elephant tusks. An odd time in her life to see a bunch of elephant tusks. She reached between the slats and touched one of them, something she had never touched before. Circus. Ringling Bros. The elephants' graveyard. Tarzan. Priceless ivory. Exotic cargo from the mysterious East. Pianos. Who'll buy my priceless ivory curios? The crate was unlabeled.

She looked across the front of the crate. Seeing no label, she went down to the next cross aisle and back to the far side of the crate, where a label had been stapled and overglued to one of the slats. The ornate script gave the name of a Hong Kong exporter; in front of the words "sold to" was typed: Penn-Harrington Industries. No! Was Harry Penn going to decorate every one of his elephant super computer memory units with an authentic, honest-to-goodness pair of elephant tusks so that each would be deserving of the name? What could it possibly mean? She wanted to laugh. "Elephant" was obviously more than just a code name. But how could elephant tusks be used in computers? Under the circumstances, it was something worth knowing.

She squatted down to examine the label. *From:* Wellington Exporters Ltd., Hong Kong. *Sold to:* Penn-Harrington Industries, San Francisco, California, U.S.A. *Deliver to:* Sun Loo Gift Shop, Clay Street and Grant Avenue, San Francisco, California, U.S.A.

"Scuse me, please."

She looked up at a young man on a lift truck. "Oh, I'm sorry if I'm in your way." She stood and backed away from the crate.

"You surprised at those? They're nothing. You're liable to see anything in this place. We opened a crate the other day had a stuffed tiger in it."

"That's something," she said. Sun Loo Gift Shop. Clay Street and Grant Avenue. Sun Loo. Clay and Grant.

He maneuvered the truck around and picked up the crate; backed up, turned, and headed for the loading platform area near the door she had entered. She watched him disappear. Then she walked back to the entrance and out into the sunshine, pausing to exchange a few pleasantries with the guard.

She returned to her car and checked the Chinatown section of her map of the city.

Beecher came for dinner, and Victoria's offering was truly splendid. As she ate the food, she reflected on how quickly she'd become accustomed to sitting down to a wonderful meal, being served, and then getting up and walking away.

Tonight, however, she was only going through the motions. She was too preoccupied to appreciate the food. Nor did she expect to appreciate using tickets provided by Harry Penn and accepted by Beecher on the same day he'd taken the third drawing of the elephant, which the technicians at Peninsula Micronics were probably poring over at that very moment, working to beat the competition at the exposition a few weeks away. Perhaps the engineers at Sturdi's firm were working from them too.

How could she justify letting her relationship with Beecher continue? Or spending an evening with Beecher even as she looked ahead to the confrontation with Penn, where she planned to spill everything?

And if she went to Penn and spilled everything, the elephant-stealing games would be over. How could she then deal with Bertini if he called again?

She looked at Beecher, who was enjoying his food. She dropped her fork in her plate and covered her face with her hands. Her shoulders shook.

"Hey, hey, now," he said. "Shake it off. Everything's finished. We can relax."

"Then why did Henry have to leave the country?"

"I told you. It's just a precaution. He's earned a vacation."

"I'm all right," she said. She wished she were. She picked up her fork and took another bite.

They drove to the Palace of Fine Arts, resplendent with the water in front of it and the wild birds. She had to keep reminding herself not to be impressed, that Diane had surely been there.

The dazzling crowd flocking to attend the San Francisco Film Festival included way-out types of every description, many "veddy British" Britishers, and crowds of what Beecher referred to as Los Angeles types. Flashes were popping all around her, and for a moment, as one flashed nearby, she thought she must be mistaking the identity of the man approaching them. Another flash, and Rex Harrison smiled at her, took her hand and nodded a greeting at Beecher. Had Diane known Rex Harrison?

The rostrum for the festivities preceding the film was shared by Harrison and Mayor Alioto and a few other notables. After the welcoming speeches and credit-bestowing speeches and show-bizzy, bouquet-throwing speeches, the stage was cleared, the house darkened, and the film shown. It was English, well acted and directed. But she found her mind wandering repeatedly during the screening. Her own problems seemed so much more dramatic.

As they were leaving, she saw a slightly familiar face. The man seemed to be middle-aged, but had a full head of youthful brown wavy hair, a dashing mustache and wire-rimmed glasses. He was dressed in a severely conservative suit. She searched her memory and couldn't place him but felt sure the pink, delicate texture of his complexion belonged to someone she knew. Then their eyes met, and the man quickly looked away. Henry Mapleway!

She forced her way through the crowd, dragging Beecher by the hand. When they reached him, he said, trying to appear as if he wasn't talking, or at least not to her, "Please. You don't know me."

"Know you! I could murder you! What are you doing here?"

"I'm sorry. You must have me confused with someone else."

She walked just behind him, half playing his little game, smiling and talking to him while appearing to talk to Beecher. "I've half a mind to reach out and pull that phony mustache right off of you. Why aren't you in England?"

"I didn't go. After Beecher dropped me at the airport, I doubled back."

"That's obvious. Why didn't you go?"

"I chose not to. Beecher convinced me I should stay out of sight. But I'm fully confident I can do it without leaving town."

"I presume you cashed in the ticket."

"I can't see that it should matter to you where I spend my little holiday, so long as I remain undercover."

"Where are you hiding out?" asked Beecher. "That is, other than at modest public functions like this?"

"I'm stopping at the Mark Hopkins. If you should need me for anything, I'm registered under the name Alexander Pope."

"Enjoy yourself on my money," she said.

"Stay away from your place," Beecher added. "And, of course, from hers. And have all your meals sent up to your room. We'll be in touch."

They stopped, and Mapleway kept walking.

"I suppose this is one problem we can't quit worrying about just yet," she said to Beecher.

"Relax," he answered. Then, as an afterthought, "Some people don't know when to accept favors."

18

She walked into the little curio shop and looked around. She saw no proprietor or other customers. A loud mechanical noise, mixed with an intermittent high-pitched whine, emanated from a back room separated from the store by a beaded curtain. She glanced at the walls lined with shelves of oriental gifts and baubles, predominantly ivory carvings. She walked around the room, examining the displays.

Working her way over to the doorway she looked through the beaded curtain. An older Chinese man was supervising a handsome young boy, also Chinese, who was cutting the elephant tusks into pieces, six to eight inches long, on a powerful bandsaw. The older man had a gaunt, unsmiling face and white hair and he wore a black jacket and striped pants and a black string-tie.

She stood, unnoticed, and watched them for several minutes as the boy worked, listening to frequent comments in Chinese from the man. The boy took the tusks, pushed them slowly through the saw, and dropped the pieces into a large green box lined with plastic. As each tusk was pressed slowly against the laboring blade, the ivory produced an ear-piercing squeal, not unlike an elephant's trumpeting. The boy had just begun. The teakwood crate was still almost full.

The proprietor glanced around finally and saw her. "Yes. May I help you?" His English was perfect.

"Oh, hello. I just wandered in to shop around and I heard the noise and wanted to see what was going on. My goodness! Look at all that ivory. Is someone going to carve up all of that ivory into pretty things?"

"All of our carvings are done in the Orient and come to us already finished. All pieces are authentic. This material is for a special purpose and will be, ah, processed in other ways." His inflection suggested a certain disdain for the intended use of the tusks.

"Processed? That sounds interesting. What sort of processing?"

"I'm afraid I don't have any idea."

"Sounds very mysterious."

"Hardly." He shrugged. "May I help you with something?"

"I'm looking for a little gift, and I thought something in ivory might be appropriate."

"Of course." He showed her around the store, pointing out the origins of certain pieces. She listened attentively and asked questions. She also listened to the bandsaw struggling through the tusks and tried to estimate how long it would take the boy to finish the job. Finally, she thanked the proprietor and left without buying anything, promising to come back as soon as she made up her mind.

Returning to Chinatown late the next day, she walked by the shop without going in. Again, no customers. She crossed the street and stood watching the store, as three ladies, surely tourists on a shopping binge, entered. Then she crossed and went in.

The proprietor smiled in recognition as she began looking around. Seeing that he was occupied with the three shoppers, she walked through the beaded curtain. The young Chinese teenager was still working. The crate was almost empty and the green box, nearly full, bore an address label printed in black ink. She watched the boy work for a moment and then went back into the store. The proprietor excused himself and left the ladies.

"I see you're still cutting up tusks," she said.

"We're almost finished." He smiled and put his hands over his ears. "I can hardly wait."

"Well, I think I know what I want." She pointed to an object in a glass case; he took it out and handed to to her. She winced at the price but bought it anyway.

She said good day to the proprietor and walked out, taking with her a mental picture of an address label—Golden State Chemical, Meade Avenue, Bayview, San Francisco—and a tiny elephant, just over three inches long, carved from ivory.

She had been to visit the small white building so many times she felt as if she worked there. She'd first come on Saturday, the morning after she'd seen the green box nearly filled with ivory in the gift shop. Expecting to find a sprawling industrial complex, she found instead an unkempt, forlorn little rectangular structure bearing a small painted sign at the entrance: Golden State Chemicals, Custom Processing.

She came back Sunday morning, on the chance that something might be happening. Relieved to find the place still deserted, she rushed home in time to go to a Forty-niners game with John Sturdi and another couple.

On Monday, she found the place open for business. While watching from her car, parked a few yards up the street, she saw a panel truck pull up to a loading dock and deliver the green box, sealed with decorative tape.

On Tuesday afternoon, her attention was immediately caught by the unusually thick, black smoke rising from a cylindrical stack on the roof of the building. She left her car, walked up to the door, and, after hesitating a moment, went inside.

She entered a small office area partitioned off from the rest of the building and approached a young girl at one of the desks.

"I'd like to see the manager," she said to the girl.

"What about?"

"It's complicated. I'd really better take it up with him."

The girl, who apparently served as receptionist, secretary, bookkeeper, and everything else required in the office, looked her up and down and said, "Go right through that door. I'm sure he'll be glad to see you."

"May I ask his name?"

"It's Ralph. He's the one in the white shirt."

"Ralph what?"

"I can't pronounce it. Just call him Ralph."

She walked through the door into the small plant. The large single room was cluttered with an assortment of grimy chemical equipment and piping. She saw Ralph in the white shirt, holding a clipboard and watching two younger men in work clothes, one of whom placed a section of ivory tusk into the hopper of an extremely noisy machine, apparently a grinder of some type. Tiny splinters and chips fell into a metal box placed beneath the machine.

The three men turned as she approached, watching her with an intensity that made her uncomfortable.

"Well, hello," Ralph said. He had a stumpy, athletic frame, light hair, heavy features, and thick, rimless glasses that made his eyes grotesquely disproportionate.

"Are you the manager?"

"Manager and owner, not that that's saying much. What can I do for ya?"

"Have you seen what's coming out of your smokestack?"

He smiled. "Smoke?"

"You can see it for quite a distance."

He shrugged. "I'm not surprised, today. What can I do for ya?"

"I'm with a group called the Committee of California Citizens for Clean Air. The CCCCA. We're a kind of vigilante group working on the pollution problem. I couldn't help noticing the black fumes you're discharging into the air."

He took off his glasses and wiped his face on his shirtsleeve. His eyes were like small glistening beads set deeply into the rolls of his face. He slipped his glasses back on and his eyes exploded back to their original size.

"Come around tomorrow," he said, "and there'll be no smoke."

"What about today?"

He turned to his two employees. "See, guys? People won't let me make a living." Then, looking back at her, "This is this one little crazy custom job. Would you believe elephant tusks?" He reached into the green box and held up a piece of the ivory. "We got a contract to pulverize this stuff, so first we have to chop it up and cook off all the organic content. That's where the smoke's coming from. It's kind of an unusual job. Rush job. But it's a one-shot deal. Most of the work I do here doesn't produce anything like this kind of smoke. Come back tomorrow and we'll be all finished and shipping this crazy business off to Indiana and the air'll be fresh and pure again."

"What on earth could this stuff be used for?"

"I couldn't say."

"You don't know?"

"Not for sure. I got some ideas. But even so, the guy that arranged this job told me to treat the whole thing very confidentially."

"Do you feel you're doing that?"

"What do you mean?" His easy look faded.

"I mean, you've already told me that you're pulverizing elephant tusks, you're cooking off the organic content first, and then you're shipping to Indiana."

"Hey, who'd you say you were?" His expression was almost hostile.

She'd taken it a little too far. "I'm only a citizen working for clean air. And having a little fun with you in the process."

"Jeez, for a minute I thought you were checking up on me. Come back tomorrow and you'll see. Everything will be perfectly ecological.

"You really should try and keep it that way. Our committee is lobbying for stronger legislation."

He winked at her. "I'll work on it."

On Wednesday she got there at nine, hoping she hadn't missed anything. Beecher had stayed late the night before, delightfully late.

She had been watching the loading platform for an hour. As Ralph had promised, the smokestack was producing nothing that might alarm an environmentalist.

An Air Express truck stopped in front of the building and backed up to the loading dock. The driver went through the front door. She slid from her car and started walking toward the building as the accordioned steel door over the loading platform began to move up into the roof. Just as she reached the loading dock, one of Ralph's helpers, accompanied by the truck driver, rolled out a small, heavy carton on a two-wheeled hand truck.

Looking down, he recognized her. He stopped and leaned on his elbows on the handles of the hand truck. "Hey, I see you came back, like Ralph suggested."

"Right. Is that the troublemaker, on the way to Indiana?"

He looked down at the box. "Sure is. We had to work late last night getting it out."

"Looks like Ralph's keeping his word," she said,

glancing quickly at the address label: *Indiana Federal, Lafayette Rd. Indianapolis, Ind.* "The air's nice and clean above your place this morning."

"Like he said, the job was a weird one. Want me to tell him you're out here?"

"No, just tell him I stopped by. And tell him I said to keep up the good work." She waved and turned and headed back for her car. She was off to Indiana.

"Hello."

She looked up from her magazine. He was perfectly recognizable as Personnel: attractive, young, neatly dressed, a warm smile, and an attentive expression.

"Hello," she said.

"My name is Bill Berdell. I understand you're looking for a job with Indiana Federal."

"That's right. I'm Diane Grant."

She got up and followed him down a short corridor and into his office. The room was spacious and the work of a decorator. He sat down in a big upholstered chair in a seating area away from the desk; she sat on a sofa.

"What brings you to us, Diane?"

"A friend suggested this might be a good place to look for a job."

"Your friend work for us?"

"No, he just knew of the company. He's in New York, which is where I was, and when he heard I was moving here to be near my parents . . ."

"Where to your folks live?"

"On . . . Lombard Street."

"Where's that?"

"It's in, I guess you'd call it, the northeastern part of town."

"He looked perplexed. "Don't know the street. Tell me, Diane. What sort of job are you interested in?"

"I'm afraid I'm just another product of an Eastern girls' school. An English major. I have no formal secretarial skills, but I do have writing experience."

"What sort of writing?"

"I spent a little time reporting for a small-town newspaper."

"Newspaper reporting." He pondered a moment. "What I'd like to do is give you a short battery of tests and evaluate them. After I have the tests and an application, I should be able to get in touch, yes or no, in a few days."

"How long do the tests take?"

"An hour."

She glanced at her watch. "Fine. But first, could you tell me a little about Indiana Federal?"

"Sure. We're major producers of a complete line of special ceramic materials used in the electronics and computer fields. Actually, they're referred to as magnetic ferrites. We turn out all sorts of little pieces that make big, impressive, modern, computer-age things work."

"Do you have any product literature, company literature, catalogs, things like that, that I might have?"

He smiled, obviously impressed by the thoroughness of her interest. "I'll have my secretary get together a folder for you while you're doing the application and the tests. I'm looking forward to going over them, Diane. And to getting back in touch." His smile this time was positively dazzling.

She smiled right back. "I'll be looking forward to that myself."

She rushed through the tests and then completed the application. Diane Grant of Lombard Street. She wondered if the phone number she listed would ring anywhere in Indianapolis.

After exchanging a little more small talk with Mr. Bill Berdell and his secretary, she left for the airport, her portfolio on Indiana Federal under her arm. She had to catch a plane back to San Francisco. She had an appointment the next morning with Harry Penn.

19

In flight to San Francisco, she went over and over the folder Berdell's secretary had prepared. An annual statement, complete with pictures of executives and the Indianapolis plant and two or three branches, including an affiliated plant in Japan. And budgetary figures. Forty million dollars in sales. And they didn't even make "things." Only little bits and pieces to go into "things."

She thumbed through the product literature and the catalog, studying the shapes and sizes of the little bits and pieces, ceramic products as Berdell called them, ferromagnetic ceramics, with their complex patterns of letter-number designations, and with specified uses, including computers. Memory-core storage elements.

The memory game again. Apparently the ivory would complete its metamorphosis at Indiana Federal and be returned to Penn-Harrington. But how? And in what form? Perhaps she'd ask Harry Penn at the appropriate moment.

She wondered what she'd say to him, what she really wanted to say, how she'd broach the subject. And sensing that she was becoming extremely tense, she ordered her allotted two martinis and found a magazine and submerged herself in a lengthy article.

Once back in San Francisco, she drove home, took a sleeping capsule and went to bed.

The tinkle of shattered glass again. A dream, a remembrance. She sat bolt upright and checked the time. Eight straight up. It had to be a recurrent nightmare, one which she had become conditioned to have on schedule, at an exact moment, involuntarily.

She heard footsteps—part of the dream. But what if it wasn't? She looked toward the door. Bertini! His two friends followed him into the room.

She screamed.

"Shut the hell up!" Bertini moved toward her.

She screamed again. And again.

He came over to the bed and slapped her with his flat hand, harder than the previous time, and she pushed her face into the pillow and cried like a child. She felt his hand grab her naked shoulder and flip her around again.

"Play time's over," he said. "We need something and we need it quick."

Victoria rushed into the room and froze when she saw the three men. The taller of Bertini's friends pointed quietly at a chair; Victoria sat down obediently.

Sitting all folded up into a clump on the bed, the

sheet pulled around her, she looked at Victoria and then back at Bertini. "Please, God, what now?" she said.

"You ain't finished yet. You got things to do and you gotta unnerstand you gotta do it today."

"That had to be the right drawing. If it's not, I don't know what to do." She broke into sobs again.

"The drawing's okay."

"Then why are you here?"

"They need a part. Not just one. A supply, a bunch of 'em. One of the things called for in the drawing. They been turning the country upside-down. Nobody knows from nothing about them. You gotta find out where they come from."

"But the deal was that I would get a drawing. And I did it."

"Well, now we're making you another deal. And so you won't think you're wasting your time, there's another piece of cake in it for ya. Okay? And this time you got one day. Unnerstand? One day. So do yourself a favor."

"But what if I can't?"

"You ain't got a choice. So figure a way, and you earn yourself another purse. If you don't, we got a problem."

"But just because you say you want them doesn't mean I'll be able to find out where you can get them." She began to cry again.

This time he hit her on the opposite side of her face, with the back of his hand. She fell over and he grabbed her hair and pulled her back up. "Don't you understand nothing?" he said. "Fun time's over. The show's in two weeks. I need the information tomorrow. The part is called IF-201. Got that? IF-201. They need at least ten thousand."

"Please let me go." The tears continued running

165

down her face. She could feel the distinct lines of pain where each finger had struck.

He slid his fingers slowly from her hair. "Ten thousand pieces. They're little. They come packed by the thousands. You could probably get ten thousand in your pocketbook. They called the logical source and they said there was no such thing. They think the logical source is lying. You find out where they come from and tell us."

She said nothing.

"You're going to see the man today," he said. "Maybe you can figure out something while you're there."

"My God," she said, softly. Then she remembered the appointment calendar on the secretary's desk. Something else to tell Penn.

"You think we don't know things?" he said. "Or call the Englishman. He's at the Hopkins, in case you didn't know." He reached into his pants pocket and brought out a grubby scrap of paper. "Here. I wrote it down. IF-201. And like I said, they need ten thousand, minimum." He dropped the scrap of paper on the table by her bed, then turned and walked out of the room and down the stairs, followed by his two lieutenants.

"Dr. Penn can see you now, Miss Lanigan."

She went into his office. Despite his very warm greeting, she felt weak, almost faint.

"I've got to talk to you," she said finally.

"You're here," he said. "You can talk to me."

"Harry—"

"Whatever it is, you know, nothing should be this upsetting."

"Harry—"

"Would you like a drink?"

She nodded.

He wheeled around in his chair and opened a compartment in the credenza behind his desk. "Scotch? Bourbon? Gin?"

"Scotch."

He took out a bottle and a glass and poured a generous shot. She drank it down, then put the glass aside.

When she finally spoke, the words came out in a rush. "Harry, I've been part of a plot to turn some of your confidential drawings over to one of your competitors."

"Well, I hope you haven't let it upset you, Ann," he said. "So have I."

20

"I'm sorry if I overdid it," he said. "Sometimes I get carried away with an impulse to do the dramatic."

"I don't know what to say next. I don't even know where to begin."

"Why not from the beginning?"

"How long have you known?"

"Since the accident."

"You know about the accident?"

"You came home after being in New York for only one day. And then your friend, I believe his name was John Hodgeson, yes, he called you and gave you the details of the accident, which you had to have already known about because it happened while you were in New York. Then, you—"

"Wait. How did you know that I was back? Or about that call? Unless—of course! You have my phone bugged!"

"You returned to New York for the funeral, and when you got back to San Francisco you told Beech your sister in New York was fine. Why would you tell him that right after the funeral? Even Beecher thought you sounded odd when he called you, though he didn't pursue it. You actually pulled it off. Even with Beecher. Tell me. What *did* happen in New York on that Friday night?"

She told him.

"Remarkable," he said. "But *why* did you do it?"

In answering the question, she found herself answering it fully in her own mind for the first time.

"I had gotten terribly bored with my own life," she said, "but there was more to it, I'm sure. Much more. Diane was very dear to me, even though I hadn't seen her for years. The accident, happening after we were finally together again, was a crushing loss. I was in a state of severe shock. I wanted desperately to have her back in the world and I remember thinking that the only way we could both exist was if I took her place. And the moment was so astonishingly—opportune."

"A gutsy thing to do," he said. "Do you regret it?"

"I guess I won't be sure for a while . . . Tell *me* something. When did you know for certain?"

"At the museum, of course. When you didn't recognize me. I knew Diane quite well, as you may have learned by now. Diane was a charmer. But you, you're amazing, the way you've pulled this thing off."

"I've wondered when I'd get caught."

"There's no reason at this point to expect you will."

"Well, *you* know about it." Something about his expression made her feel vaguely threatened by him.

"Forget that. I think you may begin to consider it a fait accompli. You see, no one noticed anything because they had no reason to be suspicious. That's what you had going for you. And it's all you needed."

"Was it enough for Beecher? I've *got* to know."

"I doubt that he or anyone else knows."

"Victoria does. I told her. I needed at least one friend. But didn't Beecher install the bug on the phone?"

"That's one he doesn't know about. I had Mapleway put it in."

"Then Henry—"

"He's heard none of the tapes. And as I said before, he's not looking for anything because he has no reason to be suspicious."

"Tapes?" Chavez! The insurance! Recorded evidence!

"The highlight of my day is coming in every morning and playing back your little exchanges with Bertini while I have my coffee. You're unbelievable. Much cooler than Diane ever was, particularly since you came into this thing blind."

"Did you know that Bertini has been knocking me around? He came this morning and hurt me . . ." She began to choke up. "He gave me an ultimatum. He said I had one day to—"

"What did he want? Some 201's?"

She nodded.

"I figured it was about time. We're not going to let them have any. We've been working on a plan to protect you and Mapleway."

"What shall I do when he comes tomorrow?"

"You won't be there. Leave everything to me. We were getting a little afraid that you'd want to hang up your trenchcoat and dark glasses, either from pressure or from conscience, before the job was finished."

"The job?"

"The whole idea has been to keep the competition off balance until the show. We've got something pretty hot, and once we get into the show with it, exclusively, we'll own a chunk of the memory game for quite a while. I'll even be able to talk back to IBM.

"The word began circulating that we had the big news a few months back. The group behind Peninsula Micronics, looking for a shortcut, came up with having Mapleway sell Diane on approaching Beecher. Henry cooperated because they were into him for some rather sizable gambling debts. And she went for it. Her rapidly developing need for money helped her rationalize what she was doing. After she approached him, Beech told me about it and I saw it as an opportunity. I decided the safest thing to do was string them along, because if they didn't think they were getting somewhere that way, they might find another way that *would* work for them. My security here is not that perfect. It's better I know just what they're up to."

"Bertini knows I'm here today," she said.

"That doesn't surprise me too much. See what I mean about my security?"

"They gave us a lot of money. You must know that."

"I like my friends to have nice things. The greater Beech's remuneration, the happier he'll be in his work. And the same goes for you. They're helping me reward you for your efforts."

"What happens when they discover they aren't getting a return on their investment?"

"We're considering a couple of possibilities. Meanwhile, we've got two more weeks to go and then we'll own the market."

"With the elephant?"

"Yes. With the elephant."

"Harry, exactly what is it?"

"It's a more efficient, higher-speed, core-storage memory concept. Based on a very bizarre secret ingredient."

"Powdered ivory, perhaps? By way of the Sun Loo Gift Shop by way of Golden State Chemical by way of Indiana Federal?"

His composure vanished. "How could you possibly know that?"

"It was a crazy fluke," she said coolly. "I was wandering along the Embarcadero last week, and happened to see the *Star of India.* I remembered hearing Beech mention *Star of India* to you, and out of some sense of coincidence, I guess, I got the guard there to let me go sightseeing in his warehouse. I found, of all things, elephant tusks. And when I looked closely, the crate had your company's name on it. So I followed it."

"You're no less than incredible. So that's why you made an overnight trip to Indianapolis."

"Which you know about because you taped my call to the airline."

"But I had no idea why you went. You know, I emphatically told Wellington to ship direct to Sun Loo and not put my name on that crate. Apparently he did it anyway."

"I still haven't any idea what you do with the ivory."

"Do you know anything about computers?"

"Not really."

"Computers must have memory-storage capacity.

This is provided by core-storage memory units which contain thousands of little doughnut-shaped pieces of ferrite, a magnetic iron oxide. The little pieces are called cores."

"And they're made by Indiana Federal."

"Among others. Here's what some ferrite cores look like." He reached into a desk drawer for a small plastic envelope containing a large number of the tiny pieces and tossed it onto the desk.

She picked up the envelope and began examining them through the clear plastic. "Just like the pictures. Almost like colorless beads, aren't they?"

"Now if you put a wire through one of them and pass a small impulse of current through the wire, the core becomes magnetized. Reverse the current, and the magnetic field in the core is reversed. In this way each core can hold two readings, like yes-no, or zero-one, the two digits in the binary numbers system used in most computer programming.

"Since each of these cores can only store a single one-or-zero bit of data, you can imagine how many thousands you need to store large amounts of information. A typical core storage unit might have a quarter of a million of these cores."

"Are these IF-201's?"

"See? You're learning already."

"Are they much different from what you'd see in other memory units?"

"Slightly smaller, but, more important, almost a thousand times faster. Now we're getting to where it all started. You might say that I'm in the elephant business today because I read a great deal to keep abreast of the market. And one of the long list of things I suffer through is the *Patent Digest*. And one day I was reading it while on vacation with Dorothy, sitting on a beach on one of the Greek islands and she was sniping at me for doing work on vacation.

"Anyway, I came across an unobtrusive little patent issued to a Joseph Nolamo, who turns out to be a retired college physics professor and one hell of an old inventor. I called Nolamo from Greece and it took two days of phoning to run him down. No one else had been in touch with him, not even IBM. Either they'd all overlooked it or failed to take it seriously. I tied him up and now own the Nolamo patent."

"And he invented the elephant?"

"Yes. You see, these little cores are produced by pressing powdered ferrite into shape and then sintering, or fusing at high temperature. The Nolamo patent teaches that if a pinch of certain calcium phosphate compounds is mixed with the ferrite before sintering, the magnetic behavior of the cores is drastically changed. He further found that of all sources of calcium phosphate, ivory from elephant tusks, which has its own unique crystalline structure, is far and away the best. Nothing else comes close. In simple terms, the elephant is a memory unit with a dash of ivory in the ferrite cores."

"So you buy ivory from the Far East, have it purified and pulverized, and then ship it to Indiana Federal and they make you IF-201 cores."

"Exactly. Now, getting back to the question of speed. The switching time, or time required to reverse the reading on a core, is expressed in microseconds, or millionths of a second, in conventional ferrite cores. It's possible with IF-201's to get switching times expressed in units called nanoseconds, or billionths of a second. In other words, a thousand times faster. Also, the cores are smaller and take smaller-gauge wire so that the entire unit is not only faster but smaller and more efficient. It gives us an edge. And a shot at the main-frame business."

"Main-frame?"

"The main unit. You see, the bulk of the computer business is owned by IBM. They get nearly all of the main frames and the little independents like ourselves and Peninsula Micronics and many others scurry around for add-on business. In other words, we make memory units which are compatible with IBM main frames.

"With the elephant we've got an advantage over the other small independents. Something to command attention as main-frame suppliers. And go for the big money. So you can see why other independents would like to get their hands on the elephant. And we'll be introducing the elephant for the first time in two weeks at the Fall Joint, the big trade exposition, so called because it's jointly sponsored by a couple of technical societies. These shows determine buying patterns. And once we show the elephant and break the publicity on it, the others like Peninsula won't be able to offer a copy of the elephant after the show because it'll be too well known that the development is ours. Their only chance is to also have it at the show and then let us spend the next ten years trying to bring them to court. That's their strategy, which should help you understand why everything is focused on introducing it at the show. I've leaked just enough rumors to get the market excited. We'll kill 'em in New York. As a matter of fact, do you know what one of my basic fears is at this point?"

"I can't imagine."

"It may sound a little presumptuous, but I'm worried about meeting the demand for elephants. Filling orders. Buyers won't wait. If we start talking deliveries of years instead of months, we've missed our opportunity."

"What do you think's going to happen?"

He smiled. "Let's have the only elephant in the New York Coliseum. Then we'll worry."

"What have the drawings been that you had me pass to Bertini?"

"The first one was the elephant with one exception. The cores specified were not 201's. They were standard, garden-variety units. And naturally it wouldn't work for them. The 201's call for different circuitry. The thing that impressed me was how quickly they checked it out. The young technicians at Peninsula are quick. Cal Tech Ph.D. types. You should have heard the way their top management explained possession of the drawings. They claimed that they negotiated for them. Then they had to explain why the drawings wouldn't work." He laughed.

"How do you know all of this?"

He smiled but didn't answer.

"Another bug. I can't believe this . . . Go ahead. What was the next drawing?"

"Next, I tried a variation we developed a year or so back which uses standard cores, a small improvement over routine rigs. We never quite got into because of the Nolamo patent. That held their interest for a while. At least it worked. But they finally decided that it couldn't be the elephant because it wasn't enough of an advance."

"And the third one?"

"The elephant. So you see, in a sense they've gotten what they paid for. But I made it more than clear to Indiana Federal that should anybody call, there was no such thing as an IF-201."

"You're playing an unbelievable cat-and-mouse game with them."

"We've got two weeks to go."

"Even if you make it, what about after the show? I can't believe they'll let up."

"You happen to be right. Having gotten into this, we've been trying to come up with a plan for handling them. But for the moment, let's win at the show."

"How did you get a bug into their plant?"

"Mapleway placed one before he became persona non grata over there. He's pretty talented. They haven't found it yet."

"Just out of curiosity, how do you know he hasn't placed one here for them?"

"He did. But he also told me so. You see, I pay him better. Occasionally we go near it and say something that sounds hot."

"How do you know he didn't tell you about one and use it as a decoy to keep you from spotting another?"

"For an amateur you've got a head like a professional. Of course we can't be sure, but we're almost sure. We limit confidential discussion to a couple of key areas around here. This office, for instance. And there are instruments that can be used for detecting bugs. And we run a sweep on the key areas every morning."

"Tell me something else. Aren't there companies other than Peninsula Micronics that might be trying to steal the elephant?"

"Any in particular you're thinking of?"

"Well, since you monitor my phone, you must know that I've met a man from one of your competitors, a man named John Sturdi, who—"

"I see you know about Marden. How did you manage that? Did you somehow find out that night at the committee meeting when Beech delivered the drawing?"

"You mean *you* know about Marden, too?"

"I'm just a poor businessman trying to keep his head above water. How did *you* find out?"

"I was cold, so I borrowed Sturdi's jacket. And I saw the envelope in his pocket when I went to the powder room."

"They're not as quick at Marden," he said, reflectively. "They've reached only the second plateau." He paused. "They're a nice group. I like John Sturdi and I was a little surprised that he approached Beecher. You know, the funny thing about all of this, the thing these guys don't know, is that the elephant is based on a most unusual ingredient. And I hold all the rights to it. I would ultimately slaughter them in court. They must figure it's a purely electronic variation and if they can get their hands on it they can bury it in their circuitry and get by."

"There's one thing about this business I still don't understand. It would seem that you could have avoided the whole thing by simply releasing the story as soon as you had the elephant. Why is it so important to tie everything to announcing at the exposition?"

"A good question. I had considered releasing the story earlier, until these guys tipped their hands by trying to steal my work. At that point I decided, if that's the way they wanted to play, fine. Business is business. You see, they banked everything on coming into the show with their version of the elephant. And they aren't going to have it. And because they've counted so heavily on it, I don't expect they'll have much else to sell. If I had released my story a long time back, they would have been forced to make adjustments and make the most of what they had. And they'd probably be a lot better off."

"Even if they got their hands on a supply of IF-201's now, isn't time about to run out on them?"

"Well, two weeks is two weeks."

"Obviously they haven't given up yet. You know what Bertini said this morning."

"They probably have nothing else to feature. You'd be amazed how much gets done the last few days before these shows."

"Couldn't they approach Beecher directly?"

"The risk is much too great. If Beecher blows the whistle on them, they're really in a mess. That's why you're so important. The extra link insulates them, gives them a margin of safety—something they could always deny. Which is why I don't believe they'd ever really harm you. Not that I'd be willing to take a chance on that."

"One more question. If I'm not going to be here tomorrow to answer the phone, where will I be?"

"He smiled. "How about two weeks on the Continent? I've had Sue make reservations for you and Mapleway to fly out of here for London today. There's just one detail that bothers me a little. They've got to be watching the Hopkins. How do we get Mapleway out of there?"

"Why don't you leave that detail to me? I've been discussing an idea with Victoria that involves getting help from some of her friends. It should work."

"I wouldn't be surprised. You know, Diane, I can hardly believe you're the same girl I knew a couple of months ago."

"The same girl? Diane?"

"Could you possibly imagine that I'd call you anything else? In a way I wish you still were Diane." His look became penetrating and warm. "Although," he added reflectively, "I knew she was beginning to fall pretty hard for Beech."

"When I came stumbling out here to start living her life, I realized there might be things I'd have to get into quickly in order to maintain the masquerade. Beecher was one—I picked up that vibration from Diane during the hour or so we spent together before the accident."

"I'm picking up the vibration that you're 'into' him yourself."

Her cheeks felt hot. "Things do have a way of happening."

He looked at his watch. "How about a quick bite of lunch? You can tell me your plan for getting Mapleway out of the Hopkins. Then you've got a busy afternoon. And after that, I'll see you in two weeks in New York."

"At the Fall Joint?"

He smiled. "At the Fall Joint."

21

Standing in the phone booth, she looked at her watch again. Another ten minutes to go before calling the taxi. It had to work one time. Just once.

After leaving Penn's office, she had driven across town to her regular gas station. She'd called the Mark Hopkins and given Mapleway his explicit instructions. He didn't argue. He seldom questioned Harry Penn's decisions and Penn had approved her plan.

Timing had to be tight, intentionally tight. Penn's reaction during lunch was to keep waiting time at the airport to a bare minimum. His travel agent had arranged all the details.

Five more minutes. The three ladies, Victoria's

friends, were at the hotel in Mapleway's room. Alexander Pope would not check out. Harry Penn would call the next day and take care of the bill. Mapleway was probably in the bathroom, changing. And voicing his objections, but complying.

Victoria was already on her way, having left the house at the prescribed time and walked down the hill with her little wheeled shopping cart, just as she did so often. She would enter a supermarket, leave without the cart by a different door, and step into a pre-arranged taxi that would take her to the airport. She would have two passports in her pocketbook and no luggage. Mapleway's passport was being picked up at his apartment by a private detective and delivered to the airline boarding area.

Time to call the special cab. Her own car was up on the grease rack, and the station would store the car until she returned.

She got into the cab. The driver made a few reckless maneuvers in and out of heavy traffic before taking the ramp onto the freeway, southbound toward the airport. In a few minutes three "ladies" would take the elevator directly to the floor below the lobby of the Hopkins. They would slip out the side door and cross the street into the Fairmont. From there, they would take a cab to the airport, where one of them would hurry to the boarding area while the other two taxied quietly back to the city.

Perhaps it was all being overdone. Mapleway in drag, taxis converging in the crowd at the airport—all of the diversionary tactics might have been totally unnecessary. It was possible that no one was watching Mapleway. Bertini might have said it for effect. But she had enjoyed giving Penn the details of her carefully thought out plan, including its contingency features. And he seemed to have enjoyed hearing about it.

At the boarding area, she found passengers waiting patiently for the door to be opened. Victoria and Lady Mapleway sat side by side, saying very little, Mapleway not terribly happy with the style in which he would be traveling. She sat down with them.

The airline attendant announced that passengers would be boarding in ten minutes. Mapleway announced that he simply had to use a rest room.

"Which one will you use?" she asked. Victoria chuckled.

Mapleway scowled through his rouge. "How could you do this to me?"

"Wait till we're on the plane. It makes no difference then."

In a matter of minutes they were on the plane and buckled into their seats in the first-class cabin. And a moment later the big jet was out to the end of the runway and then off the ground where it broke through the overcast into the crystalline afternoon air. Somewhere down in that haze, Bertini was waiting around for eight the next morning. She hoped.

The day was perfect, warm and cloudless. Not exactly commonplace for London at that time of year, or so she'd been told as she left the Connaught Hotel, where Harry Penn's agent had booked her.

She was enjoying the sun as she sat on a bench in what was already one of her favorite places in the world: a perfect little green park with Westminster Abbey to her right and Parliament in front of her, the Tower and the clock. London traffic throbbed and zipped and tooted on three sides of the park, everyone driving with a heady mania on the wrong side of the street, the funny, puffy black London taxis and the tiny English cars, so sensible and un-American, the lumbering two-storied buses and the crowds of people walking in the sun. And the pigeons, hundreds of them. This park was surely one of the world's population centers for pigeon life.

It was her first and only day to be spent in London before moving on to as many of the major attractions of Europe as two weeks allowed. Victoria had disappeared among her people as soon as they landed at Heathrow. Mapleway was with his mother for the day.

She sat quietly in the sun's warmth with her arms folded and pigeons at her feet. A man approached and sat down at the opposite end of her bench. He immediately began manipulating a portable cassette recorder, recording street sounds, playing back, and adjusting.

She watched for several minutes as he played with his expensive toy. Finally, she said, "What are you going to do? Record Big Ben?"

He turned and looked at her as if he hadn't noticed her there before, as if he might just as easily have selected any of the empty benches. "As a matter of fact, yes," he said. "In exactly two minutes."

"What for?"

"Some people take pictures."

"Oh."

A few seconds before two o'clock he turned on the recorder and held the microphone up. Once the sound was on tape, he stopped it and played it back. "How do you like that?" he said to her.

"You should have gotten a little closer."

"It's good the way I have it. Just loud enough above the sounds of the street traffic." He snapped the carrying case shut. "What brings you to London?"

"I'm running from the Mafia."

"Sure you are. And I suppose there's an important reason."

"I know too much."

"Why are you telling me? How do you know I'm not one of them?"

"Because you have natural blonde hair and a southern accent."

He grinned at her. "You like to live dangerously. When'd you get to London?"

"Yesterday."

"And how long will you be here?"

"We're leaving tomorrow for Stockholm. Have to keep moving, you know. Have to stay one step ahead of them."

"What are you going tonight?"

"Nothing yet."

"Perhaps we could have dinner."

"Love it."

"And I'll see if I can get some theater tickets."

"Love that, too."

"Look. It's early. Why don't we go and have a drink now? Or a spot of tea, if you'd prefer."

"Let's make it a drink."

"I know a perfect place, and it's not far from here." He took her arm and led her across the lawn, right by the discreet little sign that read, "Please don't walk on the grass."

Suddenly she realized that she didn't know his name. "I'm Diane Lanigan," she said, laughing. "Who're you?"

22

The Coliseum, please," she said as she settled back into the taxi. The New York traffic seemed deafening, the drivers of the huge cars intent upon running each other down.

In Europe, she and Mapleway had rocketed around the Continent, sometimes by plane but usually on the funny European trains with their comfortable compartments and their characteristic wailing whistle. She had enjoyed sitting by the window, watching the unfamiliar scenery zip by while she exchanged harmless banter with Mapleway.

He pleaded his case ardently for the first few days: "You once assured me, in fact promised me, that someday you would." "I never said that." "You most certainly did"—then, finally, accepted his role of dearest companion if not lover.

As they went from city to city, enjoying the largest hotels and the smallest, most exclusive restaurants, she kept expecting to see Bertini in every hotel lobby, perhaps even waiting in a chair in her room as she unlocked the door. " 'Course I knew where to find you. Whadda ya think? We're not as smart as Penn? We got no connections? Christ, I hadda copy of your whole itinerary. Ya see, I been taking out this tomato that works at Penn's travel agency . . ." But neither he nor anyone acting as his agent ever showed up to cause a problem.

Hoping that he wouldn't show up in New York, she paid the cab driver and hurried into the Coliseum.

The exhibition area was like a huge beehive: two floors of exhibit space swarming with people threading in and out and all through the clicks and hums and spinning discs and soundless arrays of tiny, intermittent lights, all of them moving in serious, businesslike patterns, engrossed in doing useful business.

She had gotten in with the pass from Harry Penn, but she could make no sense of the directory that listed exhibitors. As she stared down the long aisles of the main hall, the prospect of finding the Penn-Harrington space seemed hopeless.

She asked a man with a briefcase for help and learned how to use the directory, which included a layout of the exhibits. She enjoyed the moment of instruction, having picked the most attractive man in sight to ask for assistance. She smiled as she watched him hesitate before walking away, obviously wondering whether or not he should make some sort of overture.

After he left her, she easily found Penn-Harrington, the busiest area in sight. Harry Penn was talking with three men; she listened for a moment and concluded that negotiations were already at a late stage. Beecher was also busy with a potential client, and several other Penn-Harrington men were talking with visitors.

She wandered around the booth, admiring the precise detail of all the equipment on display, touching, examining, reading fine print. She half expected to find a shiny metal nameplate on one of the machines, or at least a crisp white placard in front of it, which read "The Elephant." Instead, the machines were designated by code-names, combinations of letters and numbers, CPU-40, CPU-44, CPU-48, RAM-256K. She wondered how many of the thousands walking around the show knew what she knew about the technology behind the gleaming Penn-Harrington machines, the less than one percent of something very special in the makeup of the millions of little ferrite cores. And she thought about the Embarcadero and the squealing bandsaw at Sun Loo and Ralph with the thick glasses at Golden State Custom Processing and an overnight trip to Indianapolis, where a very nice personnel man was probably still scratching his head over the strange case of Diane Grant from Lombard Street.

As Beecher's customer left, he turned and grabbed her by the back of the neck. "I'm taking you for an outstanding lunch at the world's fastest restaurant," he said. "The elephant business is fantastic, and I can't leave it for too long.

At a snack bar near the booth they had beer in paper cups and hot dogs, after which Beecher took a few minutes to show her around the exhibition. The booths were varied in size and content, some extremely large and impressive. The IBM space was the largest in sight, as large as twenty or thirty of the smaller booths. The displays were polished and striking and all of the IBM men wore dark, conservative suits and solid shirts. They went by the other giants—Burroughs, Univac, NCR, Honeywell, also solidly represented. Many of the remaining spaces were small and drab, belonging to small firms with some single component or service to offer. But she could sense that they had to be there exhibiting to stay alive.

She was fascinated by the profusion of things going on—the mechanical noises, the gleaming equipment, machines spitting out endless tongues of printed paper, rows and rows of tiny lights popping on and off in rythmic patterns. And the varying approaches to sales-manship. In some booths, all of the company representa-tives wore matching blazers. In others, fashionably slim or unfashionably curvy models handed out product literature, or greeted customers, or rattled off rehearsed product pitches, handling the barrage of leers and half-serious propositions as best they could. In still other booths, visitors sat like statues, wearing earphones, watching automatic film and slide presentations. The entire world of computer technology seemed concen-trated in that one large exhibition. She had never seen anything like it.

As they passed the nearly empty Peninsula Micronics booth, she panicked, half expecting Bertini or Croece; but Beecher assured her they would never be publicly associated with it. Walking by the Marden Microcircuits booth, she caught a glimpse of Sturdi, talking very ear-nestly to a visitor. She felt another twinge of panic and was relieved when Sturdi did not look up. They returned to the Penn-Harrington exhibit, which was, if possible, more crowded than ever. Harry Penn looked slightly harried but pleased and still in control. Penn-Harrington had the only elephant in the Coliseum, and word was apparently getting around.

Beecher immediately spotted a familiar face, a hot prospect he had worked with. He left her to go over and resume his pitch. She watched him and Penn and the others for a few minutes and then began to feel slightly drowsy. She had just flown in from Paris the night before. And she hadn't slept much. Beecher had been waiting for her.

She waved goodbye to Beecher and Penn and left. The November weather was gray but dry, and she enjoyed the walk along Central Park South toward Fifth Avenue and the Plaza. When she reached the hotel, she went right to her room and was asleep in minutes.

She was awakened by a sharp slap on her rear. "We're having dinner with Harry and Dorothy at '21,' " Beecher said. "Christ, what an afternoon! We were swamped, and in the middle of it all, Penn disappears. He's up to something, but I'm not sure what." He began taking off his clothes.

She sat up in bed. "What time is it?"

"Close to seven. We're meeting Harry and Dorothy in their suite. He's going to be transacting some business there, but he doesn't figure it'll take too long." Beecher disappeared into the bathroom and turned on the shower.

She got out of bed and went over to the window. She opened the heavy drapes and then the sheer curtains. Placing her hands on the windowsill, she leaned forward until her head touched the glass. Looking down into Central Park South, she saw two horse-drawn hansom cabs were parked in the street. Who would ride them on a chilly November evening? And how many people were down in the street or the park, staring at an undraped window in the Plaza Hotel in which a naked woman was silhouetted against the lights in the room?

She stayed for several more minutes, then went into the bathroom. Beecher stood before the mirror, a towel around his waist, and scraped at his lathered face with a razor. She touched the thick blond hair at the back of his neck, then began adjusting the shower for herself.

"You're a hell of a dish," he said. "You know that?"

"You're not half bad yourself."

"And to think," he said, somewhat reflectively, "the first time we made it was on top of a hundred grand."

The first time? She stepped quickly under the shower.

23

Dorothy Penn was sitting in a chair in the parlor of the suite shen she and Beecher walked through the door, which had been left slightly ajar. Dorothy had a highball, hardly touched, on a little table by her chair, and she was reading a *New Yorker*. A bar was set up on a small sideboard. The sound of intense conversation emanated from behind the closed bedroom door.

Beecher mixed drinks, and they sat down to talk with Dorothy and wait for the bedroom meeting to end. At one point Beecher asked Dorothy if she knew who was in there. She didn't.

At nine o'clock Harry Penn came out, looking drained, and announced that things were taking longer than he anticipated. He suggested that they go to dinner without him and save "21" for the following night. When they insisted on waiting, he made his suggestion an instruction. He took the bottle of scotch from the bar and returned to the smoke-laden room; the three of them left for the dining room in the hotel.

When they got back to the suite at ten-thirty, the bedroom door was still closed. Beecher turned on the television, and they all settled in to watch the end of a movie.

Fifteen minutes later, the door opened. Harry Penn emerged first, looking exhausted but not at all unhappy. The second person to walk out of the bedroom was John Sturdi.

Sturdi, too, looked pleased until his eyes met hers; then he looked stunned. And confused. As totally taken by surprise as she. Then, as his eyes moved back and forth between her and Beecher, his expression changed—a slightly betrayed "so that's it" look.

Two more men came out of the bedroom, one tall and one short, and Harry made the introductions. The short one's name was Dave Geddara, and he was a principal from Peninsula Micronics. She felt weak. What had the meeting been about? The tall one, Jack Hand, represented still another company, DMB Memory Systems in San Jose.

The period of time until the amenities had been satisfactorily completed seemed interminable. Finding it all but impossible to maintain her composure, particularly around Sturdi, she wanted only for the three men to leave.

"All right," Beecher said when they were finally gone. "What's going on?"

"I just put those three companies into the elephant business.

"You *What?*" she said.

"It was touch and go for a while there," said Penn. "I was afraid they might not come around to my terms."

She looked at Beecher, who seemed more interested than surprised. Apparently, he was never shocked by anything that Harry Penn said or did.

"I just don't understand," she said.

"But it's all so simple. I anticipated a favorable response here at the market. But nothing like what we've had. The CPU-48 with the five-nanosecond switching time staggers everybody—including, I might mention, IBM, who called from upstate."

"But I thought that's what you hoped for," she said.

"Of course it was. The problem is that the demand exceeds my wildest forecasts. Everybody wants elephants, and they want them next week. We could lose our whole opportunity because we can't deliver.

"When I began to see the way things were going," he continued, "and it was much more of a stampede today than yesterday, I had to think about how we could best exploit the elephant. I finally devised a plan. It consists of a coalition, or cooperative, of small independents in the Northern California area, producing main frames and components utilizing the elephant. We'll provide the technology, the design criteria, access to the IF-201's, everything they need. And then, not only do we call the shots, deciding who makes what for whom, but we charge them a stiff licensing fee for using the patent. It's a good deal for them because it guarantees them profitable business." He smiled broadly. "And it's perfect for us. Just perfect."

Beecher asked, "Do you anticipate a problem from the FTC?"

"It's possible. But we won't hear from them for a year or so, and by then we should have a fairly well established foothold. At which point we can just make those fine green licenses available to all interested parties. And there should be quite a few." The satisfied smile again.

"After all we went through to keep them from getting their hands on the elephant!" she said. "So now we end up going into business with them. It's crazy."

"Business is business," Penn said. "You see, we need them—badly. If deliveries are years off, we'll lose our advantage. Semiconductors, or something else, will start taking over. That's why this meeting tonight took so long. That guy Hand from DMB Memory was tough. He began to sense how much we needed them."

"How about the one from Peninsula Micronics?" she asked. "Was he happy?"

"I think you and Mapleway are safe. Peninsula will be realizing a nice return on their investment."

"And Sturdi? What about him?"

"Delighted. That is, until he saw you here. Serves him right."

"Business is business," Beecher said.

"Why did you choose these three companies in particular for your cooperative?" she asked.

"Well, I was familiar with their capabilities and their work, their marketing strength, that sort of thing. I liked the idea of keeping things in the Bay Area, and," he grinned, "I knew they were interested."

She shook her head. "This whole thing. I just can't get over the whole insane business."

Penn held her gaze for a moment. "Things do have a way of happening, don't they?"

"I think I need a drink," she said. "A double."

Penn glanced at Beecher. "Why not? Let's celebrate her coming to work for Penn-Harrington."

"What are you talking about?" she asked.

"I'm offering you a job," Penn said.

"She took the drink Beecher handed her. "Doing what?"

"Leave the details to me. I'll tell you when I've worked it all out."

She lifted her drink to them, then smiled. "Well, I am presently unemployed."

24

She woke up and rolled over onto her back and looked at the ceiling. Very ornate. Old hotels have very ornate ceilings. That's what's wrong with new hotels. The ceilings aren't ornate enough.

She reached over and began fingering Beecher's hair. It didn't disturb his sleeping. She gripped some of the hair and gave a gentle yank; he twitched and grunted but continued sleeping.

She snuggled her nude body up against his backside and slid an arm around his waist. "You know what I feel like doing? Right now?" she said softly into his ear.

"Later," he mumbled in his sleep.

"I feel like getting laid again."

"Later."

She pulled her arm back from around his waist and slid her hand across his naked hip and pinched his rear. "Right now."

He jumped. "Ouch! Jesus!" He held his left hand out in front of him and squinted at his watch. "Didn't we leave a call? I thought we left one. Do you know what time it is?"

"Right now."

"Fine. But this time we'll have to be quick. I've got to get over to the show. We start circulating the new word this morning."

A minute after Beecher had left for the Coliseum, she called Hertz. A quick breakfast, and she was heading up the West Side Highway and the Henry Hudson to the Sawmill, past the exit to a familiar service station, past the point where a wide grassy margin without a guardrail lay between the road and a steep embankment leading down to a railroad siding, north to the Mount Kisco exit.

When she reached the house, she pulled into the driveway. The grass hadn't been cut in almost two months. A For-Sale sign, on a wooden stake, faced the road.

She tried the front door, which was locked. The back would probably be locked, too. But the glass double doors leading from the screen porch into the dining room could be easily shaken open.

The house was totally empty. And clean. Mr. Hodgeson had surely auctioned the contents and seen that the house was made spotless for prospective buyers.

While walking from room to room, she heard a car door and went to a front window. Roger had pulled his car in behind hers and was getting out of it. She opened the front door and stepped out onto the stoop. As he looked up at her, his body sagged.

"Hello, Roger," she said quietly.

He braced himself against the side of his car.

She walked toward him. "Oh, Roger, I'm sorry if I startled you."

He managed to stand upright.

"It was unthinking of me. I should have called or sent a postcard or something."

"It's all right, really. It's just that you two always looked so much alike. So much, in fact, that—"

"You must forgive me. I just happened to be in New York for a couple of days and decided to run up and take a look at the old place."

"I understand. I saw the car in the driveway and stopped. Thought you might be a prospect."

"How are things going with the house?"

"I've had some pretty strong interest. We should have it sold fairly soon."

"I gather Mr. Hodgeson disposed of all of the furniture and all of Ann's things."

"Yes, he did. Diane . . . Would you like to have lunch? Or maybe a cup of coffee?"

"I'll have to take a rain check. I've got to get back to the city. I probably shouldn't have come, but it was the only chance I'd have."

"Surely you could take a few minutes."

"Not this time. But I'm glad I saw you, Roger."

"Nice seeing you, too. If only for a minute."

She extended her hand and he took it. Then he got into his car, backed out of the driveway, and turned left.

She backed hers out and turned right, heading for the Sawmill River Parkway and the City, for the Coliseum and Beecher Grant, for San Francisco and a job at Penn-Harrington, and for the house on Lombard Street where Diane Lanigan lived.

Communicating Today

Post

Chris Oxlade

Heinemann

LIBRARY

www.heinemann.co.uk/library
Visit our website to find out more information about **Heinemann Library** books.

To order:

 Phone ++44 (0)1865 888066

 Send a fax to ++44 (0)1865 314091

 Visit the Heinemann Bookshop at www.heinemann.co.uk/library to browse our catalogue and order online.

First published in Great Britain by Heinemann Library, Halley Court, Jordan Hill, Oxford OX2 8EJ, a division of Reed Educational and Professional Publishing Ltd. Heinemann is a registered trademark of Reed Educational & Professional Publishing Ltd.

OXFORD MELBOURNE AUCKLAND JOHANNESBURG BLANTYRE
GABORONE IBADAN PORTSMOUTH NH (USA) CHICAGO

Designed by Visual Image
Illustrations by Visual Image
Originated by Ambassador Litho Ltd.
Printed in Hong Kong/China

05 04 03 02 01
10 9 8 7 6 5 4 3 2 1
ISBN 0431 11374 2

British Library Cataloguing in Publication Data

Oxlade, Chris
    Post. – (Communicating today)
    1. Postal service – Juvenile literature
    I. Title
    383

Acknowledgements

The Publishers would like to thank the following for permission to reproduce photographs:
Aviation Images: p21; Canon Printers: p25; Corbis: p28, Colin Garratt p20, Tim Hawkins p12, Matthew McKee p7, Minnesota Historical Society p4, Paul Seheult p5, Patrick Ward p6; Parcel Force: p5; Philip McCollum: pp13, 22; R.D. Battersby: p26; Royal Mail: pp14, 15, 17, 19; Sheena Verdun-Taylor: p27; The Stock Market: p23; Stone: Bob Schatz p24, Lawrence Migdale p4; Tudor Photography: p8; US Postal Service: p18.

Cover photograph reproduced with permission of The Royal Mail.

Every effort has been made to contact copyright holders of any material reproduced in this book. Any omissions will be rectified in subsequent printings if notice is given to the Publisher.

CONTENTS

Any words appearing in the text in bold, **like this**, are explained in the Glossary.

COMMUNICATIONS

Communications are ways of sending and receiving information. Important ones include television, radio, telephone (and **fax**), the **Internet** (and **e-mail**), post and newspapers.

This book is about post. It examines how items of post such as letters and parcels get from where they are posted to where they are delivered, the technology that postal services use, and the people they employ. It also looks at other jobs that some postal workers often do, such as handling **licence** applications, as well as at the effect that the growth of e-mail is having on postal services.

What is post?

Post is a way of sending a letter, packet or parcel from one place to another. Post is an important form of communication because it allows us to send messages and objects cheaply and simply, without needing any special technology of our own.

A postal worker on her 'round' or 'walk'. This is the last stage in the long journeys of the letters and parcels she is carrying.

Postal services make wide use of modern technology. This worker is scanning a **barcode** so that the progress of a parcel is tracked as it moves through the postal system.

Post is collected, sorted, transported and delivered by postal services. Different countries have postal services that are organized in different ways and that use different words for their services and operations. However, the work they do is quite similar. The quantity of post they handle is extraordinary. The USA has the world's busiest postal system – it delivers more than 200 billion items of post every year. That's an average of more than 6000 items per second!

As it explains how postal services work, this book looks at how two sample items might travel from one person to another. These are: a letter sent by the **standard service** from the UK to the USA, and a parcel sent by parcel post from the USA to Australia.

POSTAL SERVICES

The majority of countries in the world have a postal service that is operated by their government, or that is operated for the government by a private company. Postal services are huge and complicated organizations. In most countries they are made up of two parts. The first part is a **network** of **post offices** where people take items of post to be posted, have them weighed, and buy stamps and stationery. The second part is an organization that collects, sorts, transports and delivers the post through a network of **sorting offices**.

Large sorting offices, such as those that handle the post in business areas of large cities, process hundreds of thousands of items of post every day. As much work as possible is done by specialized machines that transport and sort the post, but many postal workers are still needed. For example, the US Postal Service employs nearly 800,000 people.

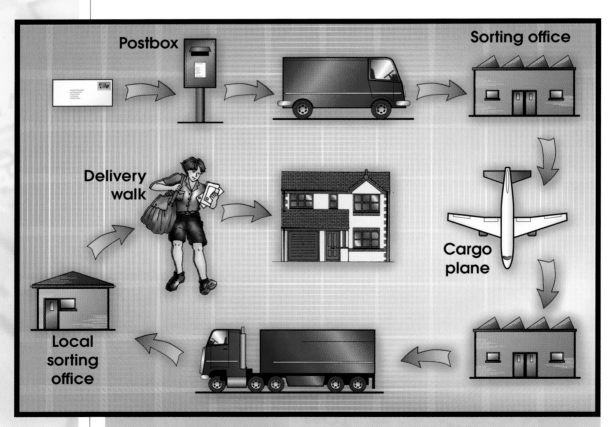

This diagram shows the possible stages in the journey of a letter as it is carried from its sender to its recipient through the postal system.

Postal workers sorting letters by hand at a local sorting office.
Post for different groups of houses is put together in different
pigeon holes.

The postal route

Our sample letter begins its journey in the UK. The sender drops
the letter into a postbox on the street. At certain times of day
the letter, along with any other letters in the box, is collected.
It is taken to a nearby sorting office, along with thousands of
letters collected from other postboxes and post offices. At the
sorting office, all the letters are sorted into groups, depending
on their destination.

Our letter goes into a bag with other letters addressed to
overseas countries. It is transported to an airport and to the USA
by **cargo plane**. On arrival it is sorted with letters arriving from
other countries. The groups of letters from sorting offices are
transported to a local sorting office near their destination.
Here they are sorted again, ready to be delivered to houses
and businesses.

Our sample parcel starts its journey to Australia at a post office
in the USA. It travels in a similar way to the letter, via sorting
offices, along with thousands of other parcels.

7

POSTAL PRODUCTS

There is a wide range of postal services that customers can choose from. There are services for different sizes and weights of items, for different speeds of delivery and for different destinations (the same country or overseas). Each service has a different cost. Normally, the heavier the item and the faster the delivery, the higher the cost.

Standard and express

Most items of post are sent by the **standard service**, or letter post. In different countries this service has different names and may have two or more different classes for different speeds of delivery. For example, in the UK, letters can be sent by first-class or second-class post.

Most postal services also offer an express mail or priority mail service that guarantees an item will arrive the next day, or perhaps within two days in a large country. Express services cost more than standard service. With recorded or special delivery services the person who receives the item signs to say it has arrived. Items sent by this sort of service can often be insured in case they are lost or damaged en route.

Letters and small packets sent using various postal services. They include pre-paid envelopes and packets, and stamped and franked items.

In remote areas of the world, small amounts of post are transported over long distances. This plane is collecting post in the Australian outback.

Prohibited by post

There are some restrictions on what can be sent in the post. Some items are not allowed because they are potentially dangerous or unpleasant for postal workers who handle them. These include dangerous chemicals, explosives, poisons, batteries and bottled gases.

Business services

Postal services often offer extra services for businesses that want to do **mailshots** to customers or potential customers. Businesses can supply the postal service with items that are addressed and already sorted into bundles ready for delivery, and can get a discount on the cost. They can also have brochures delivered to all the addresses in a particular area by the postal service.

Courier services

Courier companies are private companies that collect and deliver packages and parcels. National and international courier companies operate delivery **networks** similar to the postal networks, but handle far fewer items. Every item is identified with a **barcode** so that its journey can be tracked from start to finish.

PREPARING TO POST

To make sure that items will be delivered to the right place at the right time, they must be properly prepared. All items must have the address of their destination clearly written on them, and parcels must be carefully packaged.

Postcodes

To help with the organization of deliveries, most countries are divided into postal areas. Each area has its own **postcode**, made up of digits or a combination of letters and digits. For example, the US Postal Service uses five-digit or nine-digit codes (known as 'ZIP' codes); in the UK the Royal Mail uses a two-part code that combines letters and numbers; Australia Post uses a four-digit code. The postal service uses its postcodes to send items to the destination **sorting office**, from where they are finally delivered. Rural postcodes might cover several villages, but city postcodes can cover an area as small as one office block or even a floor of an office building.

Writing the postcode clearly is important so that workers and machines at sorting offices can use them to sort the mail. Our letter is going to the USA, so it needs a US ZIP code written on it. Our package needs an Australia Post postcode on it.

It is important to clearly address any item that is to be posted. This address includes a US ZIP code. A barcode can be seen at the bottom of the envelope.

Weighing and paying

Once an item has been weighed and a service chosen, the cost of sending it can be worked out. Post is normally paid for in advance in one of three ways. The first is with stamps. The second is by **post meter** or **franking machine**. This is rented from the postal service and prints a postmark and amount paid on to the item. The third is by using **pre-paid envelopes**.

Both of our sample items are paid for with stamps attached to them. The letter goes by first-class post, which is always carried abroad as **airmail**. An airmail sticker is stuck on the front. The parcel can go by airmail or by the much slower and cheaper service of surface mail (which transports items by road, rail or ship). In this case, the sender chooses airmail.

Special-issue stamps from Australia, the UK and the USA. Postal services issue these picture stamps to celebrate special events or aspects of their country.

COLLECTING POST

Our sample letter is dropped into a postbox in the middle of the day. A postbox slot is narrow so that a letter can be dropped in but nobody can reach inside and pull other people's letters out again. During the day, as other people post their letters or small packets, post gradually piles up inside the postbox. The boxes outside **sorting offices** or busy city-centre **post offices** may have a conveyor belt at the base that carries the post away. This stops the box becoming too full. There is a locked door in the side of postboxes that postal workers can open to collect the post.

Our sample parcel is handed to a member of the counter staff at a post office in the middle of the afternoon. It is put in a container with other parcels that have been handed over that day.

Large businesses and organizations often have their own post departments that collect post and put it in large containers ready to be loaded into vans from the sorting office.

The slot in the postbox is designed to stop people reaching in to steal post. The notice on the front of the box gives information about collection times.

To the sorting office

Vans from the sorting office make regular visits to postboxes and post offices. A notice on a postbox and at the post office says when collections are going to be made so that people can post their items in time. In towns and cities there may be three or four collections every day. In rural areas there might be just one collection at the end of the day. Our sample letter and parcel arrive at sorting offices at the end of the afternoon.

Collecting from the customer

Some postal services offer package delivery services similar to those offered by **courier** companies. The sender orders the service and a postal worker collects the package, and writes down the sender's name, address and the destination address on a document called a **waybill**. The postal worker regularly returns to the sorting office with newly collected parcels.

A customer hands over a parcel at a post office in the USA. The customer pays the fee for sending the parcel at the same time.

SORTING OFFICES

From **sorting offices**, our letter and parcel, along with all the other letters, packets and parcels that have been collected, will be carried to delivery sorting offices near their destinations. The first job is to sort this post into piles of items that are addressed to places near each delivery sorting office. This is a complicated job, and a huge one at a city sorting office where hundreds of thousands of items of post arrive every day. Many of the sorting tasks are done by machines, but thousands of postal workers are needed to sort by hand, move post around and load it into and out of vans and trucks.

Moving machinery

A sorting office has many different machines to move post around. They include machines for handling individual letters, packets or parcels, sacks of post and large containers of post. Individual items and sacks are moved automatically by conveyor belts, sloping **chutes** and **roller tables**. Containers or sacks full of parcels are towed by hand or by small tractors, and lifted on and off vans by fork-lift trucks.

Mixed post (containing letters and packets of many shapes and sizes) arriving at a sorting office from postboxes and **post offices**.

This is the inside of a sorting drum. As the drum spins round, letters and thin packets drop through the slots, leaving only thicker packets and parcels inside.

Letter, packet or parcel?

Our letter and parcel arrive at a sorting office mixed in with thousands of other letters, packets and parcels of many different shapes and sizes. The first stage in sorting is to separate these items into standard-sized letters, larger items of flat post, small packages and larger parcels. Standard-sized letters, such as our letter, can be sorted by machine – so they are called **machineable** items. Other items, like our parcel, are normally sorted by hand. The first stage of separating letters from larger items is done by a large rotating drum. It has slots in it that let the letters fall through, but not the packages and parcels.

PREPARING TO SORT

After being divided from the other post, **machineable** letters, including our letter, travel to machines that prepare them for sorting by other automatic machines. The other post, including our parcel, goes to a different area of the **sorting office**, ready to be sorted by hand.

Facing and cancelling

The first two stages in preparing letters for sorting are called facing and cancelling. Most stamps have **fluorescent** ink in them that the human eye cannot see, but which a facing machine detects. The machine turns the letters so that the stamps are face up and at the top. Then a cancelling machine prints a postmark over the stamps to show that the letter has been collected. The postmark shows the date and name of the sorting office.

Postcoding

The next stage is to mark a machine-readable code on the letters to tell the sorting machine which route the letters must take to reach their destination. The code is often a **barcode** or pattern of dots, again containing fluorescent ink. Once the code is on the letters, the letters can be quickly sorted by machines nearer their destination.

Part of a cancelling machine at a sorting office. The letter on the right has just had a postmark printed on it and is joining a pile of postmarked letters.

The most up-to-date coding machines have computer technology, and can read the **postcode** on each letter using special **software**. The machine sends a video picture of the address to the computer, and the computer works out which part is the postcode and identifies the characters in the code. Some machines can read the address too, check that the postcode is correct, and change the code if necessary! Other coding machines are semi-automatic. An operator reads the postcode and types it into the machine.

Our letter and parcel are both addressed to overseas destinations (the USA and Australia) and have overseas postcodes, which means they cannot be coded for automatic sorting until they arrive in those countries.

On this coding machine, writing that the machine cannot recognize is shown on a screen for the operator to try to read instead.

SORTING MACHINES

Once letters have been marked with a machine-readable sorting code they are passed to the sorting machine itself. A stream of letters enters the machine, which reads the codes and guides the letters to one of dozens of different containers. From here they will be loaded into vans and trucks that will carry them to their destination sorting offices.

Barcodes are read by a barcode scanner, just like the one at a supermarket checkout. **Dot codes** are read by a similar system that detects the pattern of dots. The code is passed to a computer, which looks up in a table the destination group for the letter. The computer sends this information back to the machine. The machine moves a set of flaps which direct the letter to the correct container. This process happens at very high speed. A single sorting machine can sort 35,000 letters per hour. That's ten letters every second.

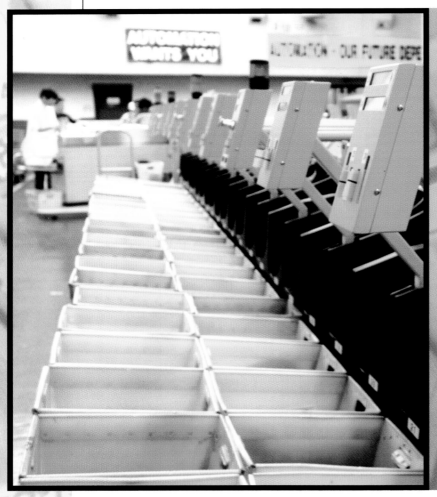

Rows of containers are filled with letters from the sorting machine. Each container collects letters for a particular destination.

Sorted post is loaded into wheeled bins or trolleys. Then it is taken to the sorting office's loading bay and rolled into trucks.

If the postal service decides to change the routes that post takes to different **sorting offices**, it can do it by changing the **software** on the sorting machine's computer.

Non-**machineable** items of post, such as packets and parcels, are difficult to sort by machine because they come in so many different shapes and sizes. They are normally put on a large sorting table surrounded by containers or sacks, one for each destination. Postal workers sort them into containers by hand.

The containers and sacks of sorted post are labelled with codes. Postal workers can then tell to which destination office all the items inside are going.

Parcel sorting

Some postal services have equipment that can sort large barcoded parcels such as ours automatically. Specialized 'wide-area' barcode scanners read a barcode wherever it is on the parcel. As the parcels move along a conveyor, they are sorted on to other conveyors by mechanical arms. The conveyors carry the parcels straight to waiting vans and trucks.

TRANSPORTING THE POST

Postal services operate huge transport fleets to collect post, move it quickly between **sorting offices** and deliver it. Organizing postal transport is a complex job that is handled by a special department of the postal service, or by an outside **contractor**. Apart from deciding the routes needed for efficient distribution of the post between sorting offices, postal services have to hire drivers, pilots, maintenance staff and workers to load and unload vehicles at railway and road terminals, airports and ports.

Long distance and local

Our letter, along with other overseas post, is carried by truck from the sorting office to a post centre at an airport. Sacks and containers for different countries and regions are loaded on to **cargo planes**, normally operated by private **cargo carriers**. The container with our letter inside is loaded on to a plane for its journey to the USA. On arrival in the USA, the container is taken

In many countries, a lot of mail is sorted on special mail trains as it travels between major sorting offices. This saves sorting time when the post arrives in the right area.

to a sorting office. Here the post inside the container is coded and sorted. It can then continue its journey through the US postal system by plane and truck.

A similar thing happens to our parcel. It is carried by truck to an airport post centre, where it is loaded on to a cargo plane with other parcels for Australia. It arrives a day later and is sorted for its onward journey by Australia Post.

Local collections and deliveries are made with vans, motorcycles, bicycles and hand carts. In the remote rural areas of some countries post arrives only once a week. Sometimes it is carried by pack animals such as camels.

Loss and damage

Postal services collect and deliver millions of items every day, so it is not surprising that some items occasionally get lost or damaged. This can easily happen if a train or plane breaks down or is diverted by bad weather. By paying a small fee, senders can insure their items against loss or damage, or against late arrival.

A cargo plane belonging to the US postal service is loaded with containers full of letters and parcels, for delivery across the country.

DELIVERING THE POST

Eventually, our letter and parcel arrive at their destination **sorting offices**, from where they will be delivered to the address written on them. Letters and small packets are delivered in walks or rounds. The person who delivers the post walks or cycles along a pre-set route, delivering to all homes and offices along it. Parcels are delivered by truck or van.

Sorting into walks

The post that arrives at a local sorting office is sorted into groups, one for each walk. Then the post for each walk is put into the correct order for the walk and loaded into **pouches** ready for delivery. On long walks, there may be too much post for the deliverer to carry. In this case a van is used.

At small sorting offices, items are sorted by hand. The workers who sort them have to remember which streets or businesses are on which walk. At larger city-centre offices, post is sorted automatically by machine.

A postal worker using a van to deliver post. Workers normally do the same round everyday because they know the street names and house numbers.

Our letter is sorted into a group with other letters to be delivered to homes and businesses on the same walk. It arrives in the middle of the day, two days after it was posted in the UK. Our parcel is loaded on to a delivery truck with other parcels for the same area. It is finally delivered to the destination written on it, four days after it was posted in the USA.

International post

Both our letter and parcel have been posted in one country but delivered in another. The sender has paid the postal service in the first country, but work has been done by the postal service in the other to deliver it. So how does the second postal service get paid by the first? The answer is that it doesn't. All postal services are members of an international organization called the Universal Postal Union. Each member delivers post paid for and sent from overseas free of charge. This expense is balanced by the fact that they don't have to pay for the delivery of items they send overseas.

A parcel arrives at the end of its journey. The girl is signing a form to say that she has received her parcel from the postal worker.

POST AND THE INTERNET

Many types of message that used to be sent through the post are now sent electronically. They are sent as **fax** messages, over the **Internet** as **e-mail**, or directly from computer to computer. For example, simple letters can be sent in seconds by e-mail, information can be looked up on the Internet rather than by ordering brochures to be sent by post, and people in different offices of the same company can exchange information through computer **networks**. So why do we need postal services at all?

The need for post

Postal services and **couriers** will always be needed because many items cannot be sent electronically. In fact, the amount of post dropped into postboxes around the world is still growing. This is mainly because of the increase in a type of post called **direct mail**, which companies send to the public to try to persuade them to buy their products. The number of parcels being sent by couriers is also rising as more people order goods over the phone or the Internet instead of going to the shops and carrying them home themselves.

This women is ordering goods over the Internet from a shopping website. The postal service is needed to deliver her goods.

Postal services on the Net

Postal services and courier companies use the Internet to help them deliver post more quickly and cheaply to their customers. For example, companies buy postage for their **post meters** or **franking machines** over the Internet, and **postcodes** can be looked up and checked through postal service **websites**. Some postal services allow customers to buy stamps on the Internet, which they can print out at home.

An item of post sent by special services has a **barcode** attached to it. The code is scanned at each stage of the item's journey so that a central computer knows where it is. The sender can track the item's progress on the service's website.

Remote printing

Some postal services also offer a service called electronic distribution. Companies send their advertising brochures to **sorting offices** by e-mail, where the brochures are printed, addressed and sorted, ready for delivery.

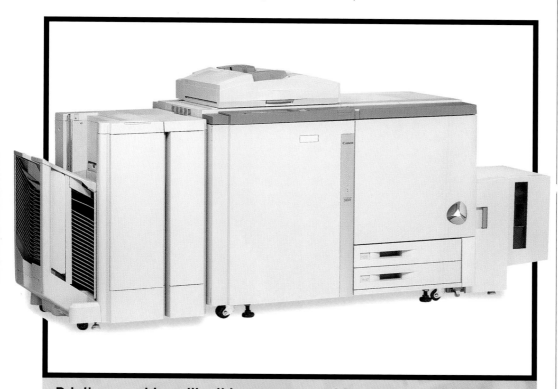

Printing machines like this one are used by postal services for electronic distribution. Brochures and other pamphlets are printed at the sorting office from where they are delivered.

POST OFFICE NETWORKS

Postal services are made up of a delivery **network** that collects, sorts and delivers post, and **post offices** where customers take their post to be weighed, and buy their stamps and packaging materials. In most countries, there is a network of thousands of post offices, and they offer many other services, such as banking and issuing various **licences**. In some countries, post offices are combined with local shops.

Post office services

In many countries post offices are operated, or were originally operated, for the government. Apart from handling post, some also carry out other functions for the government. In the UK these functions include issuing payments such as **unemployment benefit** and **pensions**, and handling passport and driving licence applications. Postal services are usually very efficient at distributing post, so they are naturally good at distributing other items, too. In some countries they even help with the distribution of medical supplies to remote areas.

In some rural areas, the post office can be the centre of village life. Many sell groceries as well as providing a wide range of other services.

Post offices may also offer their own banking service, which many people in remote areas use because there are few bank branches close by. At such post offices, people can also pay their bills at the post office counter.

Carrier alerts

The postal workers who deliver post to homes gradually get to know the people they deliver to, and notice such things as who is in and out when they visit. In some countries, including Australia, the deliverers look out for out-of-the-ordinary things, such as post piling up in a letterbox, which may mean the resident has collapsed, for example. If they notice anything unusual, they call the police. This is called a carrier alert.

A customer talking to a member of the counter staff in a post office. The staff are trained to deal with all the different services that the post office offers.

POST TIMELINE

Here are some of the major events and technical developments in the history of post.

2000 BC — Earliest records show postal services exist in Ancient Egypt. Messages are carried by people on foot or horseback.

1st century AD — The Roman Empire has an efficient postal service that carries messages from Rome to the furthest corners of the huge empire. The service is called the *cursus publicus*. Its messengers ride on horseback between postal relay stations on the road **network**.

13th century — Several postal systems are set up in Europe and used by merchants for business correspondence. At this time, most people cannot read or write, so they have no need for a public postal service.

1627 — A public postal service with **post offices** opens in France.

1635 — A similar service opens in England.

A rider of the Pony Express mail service in the USA. This photograph was taken in about 1861.

1840 In the UK, Rowland Hill introduces a new postal system that uses stamps for the first time. The cost is the same no matter how far the destination.

1860 The Pony Express is introduced in the USA. Riders on fast horses carry small packages and letters between relay stations, where they collect fresh horses. Average speed is about 300 kilometres (200 miles) per day.

mid-19th century The development of railways and steam ships speeds up long-distance post and international postal services. On the railways, mail trains with **sorting offices** had been introduced in 1838.

1875 General Postal Union (international postal organization) is formed – today called the Universal Postal Union.

1918 A regular **airmail** service begins to operate in the USA.

1919 An international service links London and Paris.

1939 Transatlantic airmail services begin, using 'flying boats' (boats that can take off from and land on water).

1960s Electronic post handling and sorting systems are introduced.

1963 The ZIP **postcode** system is introduced in the USA.

Loading mail on to the first flight of the US Post Office's airmail route between St Louis and Chicago, in 1926.

GLOSSARY

airmail post which is carried by plane

barcode set of narrow black-and-white lines. The pattern made by the different widths of the lines is a code that represents a set of numbers.

cargo carrier company that transports cargo, in this case post, in return for a fee

cargo plane plane designed for carrying post and parcels

chute sloping slide that letters, packets and parcels automatically slide down

contractor company that works for another company or organization

courier person or organization that delivers packets and parcels in return for a fee

direct mail type of advertising that companies send to people through the post

dot code pattern of dots which can be read by a machine which sorts letters

e-mail short for electronic mail, a system that allows people to send written messages to each other's computers via the Internet. Also the name given to a message.

fax system that allows a copy of a document (containing text and pictures) to be sent along a telephone line

fluorescent describes a substance that gives off light when it is hit by certain types of radiation

franking machine machine rented from the postal service that stamps a postmark on an item of post

Internet global computer network that allows people with computers linked to it to access information on any other computer around the world, and to exchange e-mails with other people with computers

licence document that says a person is allowed to do something, for example, drive a car

machineable describes a letter or packet that is small enough and flat enough to be sorted automatically by machine

mailshot to send the same brochure or leaflet to all the addresses in an area. Businesses use mailshots for advertising.

network chain of interconnected systems, for example, the postal network is made up of linked sorting offices

pension money paid to people who have retired from full-time work

post meter machine rented from the postal service that stamps a postmark on an item of post

post office building where people go to post letters, packets and parcels, buy stamps and pay for postal services

postcode code of digits and letters given to a particular area by a postal service

pouch small bag

pre-paid envelope envelope on which the postage is paid as part of the price of the envelope itself. No stamps are needed to post it.

roller table table in a sorting office with rollers in the top. The rollers make it easy to push heavy parcels along the table during sorting.

software computer program

sorting office building where post is collected together and sorted into groups for different destinations

standard service service by which most letter post travels in a country

unemployment benefit money paid by a government to people who have no job and so do not earn money

waybill form that shows the details of a parcel, such as its weight, contents, sender and recipient

website collection of information stored on a computer that anybody with a computer connected to the Internet can look at

INDEX

Titles in the *Communicating Today* series:

Hardback   0 431 11375 0

Hardback   0 431 11370 X

Hardback   0 431 11374 2

Hardback   0 431 11371 8

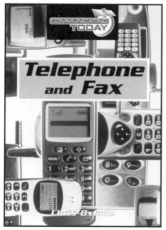

Hardback   0 431 11373 4

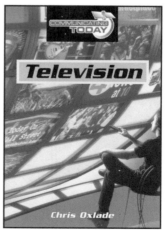

Hardback   0 431 11372 6

Find out about other Heinemann resources on our website www.heinemann.co.uk/library